UNDEFEATED

CATCHING INSPIRATION AND HOPE
THROWN BY ATHLETES OF INTEGRITY

DAVE BRANON

BETHANYHOUSE

MINNEAPOLIS, MINNESOTA

Published by Bethany House Publishers
11400 Hampshire Avenue South
Bloomington, Minnesota 55438

Bethany House Publishers is a division of
Baker Publishing Group, Grand Rapids, Michigan.

Printed in the United States of America

ISBN-13: 978-0-7642-0293-3
ISBN-10: 0-7642-0293-6

Library of Congress Cataloging-in-Publication Data

Branon, Dave.
    Undefeated : catching inspiration and hope thrown by athletes of integrity / Dave
Branon.
       p. cm.
    Summary: "Collection of inspirational biographies of more than thirty-five top athletes.
Intended for sports fans ages twelve and older"—Provided by publisher.
    ISBN-13: 978-0-7642-0293-3 (pbk.)
    ISBN-10: 0-7642-0293-6 (pbk.)
    1. Athletes—Conduct of life—Juvenile literature. 2. Athletes—Biography—Juvenile
literature. 3. Role models—Juvenile literature. 4. Sports—Juvenile literature.
5. Christian life—Juvenile literature. I. Title.
    GV697.A1F724   2006
    796.04'40922—dc22
    [B]   2006019414

UNDEFEATED

In memory of my daughter Melissa,
who graced our lives for seventeen years,
making each day better just because she was here.

DAVE BRANON is managing editor of the award-winning magazine *Sports Spectrum,* which has led to his writing numerous sports books, including *Heads Up!, First & Goal,* and *Slam Dunk.* In addition to sports writing, Dave has developed a loyal following among the millions of readers of the devotional guide *Our Daily Bread.* Dave is married to Sue and lives in Grand Rapids, Michigan.

CONTENTS

DO NOT UNDERESTIMATE THE POWER OF ATHLETES TO INFLUENCE LIVES.

I remember coming under the spellbinding power of an out-of-this-world basketball player when I was in college. This guy was, in my book, the best player on the planet.

He was pure magic—performing sleight-of-hand tricks with a basketball that no basketball fan had ever seen. His passing and dribbling prowess was right out of the handbook for how to become a Harlem Globetrotter.

And could this man shoot! Not just jump shots, but running one-handers and slashing lay-ups. He was a one-man offensive show that had fans standing in line to watch.

Pete Maravich held me in awe. As a small-college player at the time of his big-time showmanship at Louisiana State University, I could not get enough of him. I studied what he did, hoping to become one-eighth the player he was.

He was, in almost every sense, my hero.

However, there was one thing about Pistol Pete that I did not emulate—and could not emulate. While I was enamored with Pete Maravich the basketball player, I was not as fond of Pete Maravich the person.

While I copied his moves on the court, I did not want to be like him the rest of the time. He sulked. He was angry. He drank too much. He wasn't especially nice to people.

As a hero, he was a great basketball player but a poor role model.

Even as he moved on to the pro ranks, his lack of discretion in life escalated. Indeed, the Pistol was a lost and pathetic person who had grown up thinking that success in basketball and getting rich off the game would bring happiness.

It was not until after his career ended that Maravich finally did what he had not done when he was eighteen and heard the gospel clearly presented. After he retired from the game and had tried everything he could think of to gain happiness, he finally gave his life to Jesus Christ.

When he did, he completed his role as someone who could be emulated. After his salvation, he became an on-fire Christian who couldn't be stopped. He toured the country talking about Jesus. Only then was he able to be a hero both on the court and off. Only then could his life become a beacon of hope, showing others how to live and how to love God.

Today, when you look over the landscape of athletes to respect and emulate, it's encouraging to know that there are men and women who can be respected for both their athletic ability and their spiritual wisdom.

Those are the kinds of athletes whose stories are told in *Undefeated.* Each of the men and women in these pages has demonstrated tremendous God-given talent in his or her sport, but has also shown how to live by biblical principles.

Each has lived out a godly principle in at least one aspect of life, making his or her life itself a testimony to the value of following the standards and guidelines of the Bible.

Just as I admired Maravich for his skills, we can be amazed by what these athletes have done. And just as I saw Maravich's transformed life demonstrate how to live for Jesus, we can be challenged by the clear ways they live by the Word.

For the Christian sports fan, it's the best of both worlds: top skills and godly living. And isn't that the way we should all approach life?

Wendy Ward
Moment of Integrity, Lifetime of Testimony
The man of integrity walks securely,
but he who takes a crooked path will be found out.
—*Proverbs 10:9*

BEING HONEST COST WENDY WARD MONEY. A lot of money.

Wendy Ward knows about winning a lot of money at golf tournaments. For instance, in 2001, she won the Wendy's Championship for Children (not named after her but after the famous restaurant chain). That victory was her third LPGA championship. In her career, which began in 1994, she has won more than $3 million. Wendy knows how to win.

But one Sunday afternoon in 2000, her honesty and her belief in following Jesus and trusting His standards for living cost her at least the chance for first-place money in another tournament.

She and her playing partner, Juli Inkster, were in a showdown for first place at the McDonald's LPGA Championship—a major on the LPGA Tour. And anyone who can spell the name Phil Mickelson knows how important it is for a golfer to win a major. It is an automatic stamp of credibility for a professional golfer's career.

On this particular Sunday, the two veteran golfers entered play tied for first place after fifty-four holes. In the final round, they battled through each hole, and as they made the turn into the last nine holes, both the tournament title and a hefty check were up for grabs. The way they were knocking down shots, either woman could easily walk home that day with the big money.

On the thirteenth hole, Ward smacked a shot onto the green, a shot that landed her ball within easy striking distance for par. She grabbed her putter and walked onto the green. She stood over the ball, held her putter in place, and prepared to hit the ball. It was just a ten-footer—pretty much a gimme that would have allowed her to maintain her position in her battle with Inkster.

But before she could coax the ball into the cup, an odd thing happened. The ball moved. On its own. She hadn't hit it or brushed it. It just moved. Who knows why?

Now, if you and I were playing, neither of us would probably know that this kind of thing can be a problem. We'd probably laugh it off, saying, "Hey, did you see that? My ball moved!" We'd exchange a chuckle with our playing partner, and then we'd go ahead and putt the thing in.

But Wendy knew the rules. She knew that if the ball moved—for any reason—after she had addressed it, she had to assess herself a one-stroke penalty.

Here's the thing. No one else saw the ball move. Not even her playing partner, Juli, had seen it make its mischievous move.

Nobody saw the ball do its little wiggle but Wendy.

And God.

She could have proceeded as if nothing happened. She could have pulled her club back and tapped the shot into its little resting place.

But she didn't. Instead, Wendy told Juli that the ball had moved. Then, doing just as the rules required, she added another stroke onto her own score.

That's like Shaquille O'Neal waving off his own basket because he knew he traveled but no one else noticed.

"Hey, ref! Forget that dunk I just threw down. I took an extra step back there!"

Or Roger Clemens yelling to the ump, "Hey, Blue! You called that a strike, but you know what? I balked right while I took my stretch, and you didn't see it. Better change that to a ball and send the guy down to second."

That'll happen about as often as the Chicago Cubs win the World Series.

So Wendy assessed herself that extra stroke. Then she missed the putt. Suddenly she was staring down the barrel at a double bogey.

This wasn't just any stroke Wendy was giving up. As play went on, she and Juli kept battling—until Inkster won the final hole, and when she did, Inkster and Stefania Croce ended up with a 281 to force a playoff for the big money.

And how did Wendy Ward finish? You guessed it! She went into the clubhouse with a 282—just one self-assessed penalty stroke behind the co-leaders.

Inkster won the tournament in the playoff and took home a nifty check for $210,000.

She recognized Ward's show of true sportsmanship. Of her playing partner, the champion said, "What Wendy did shows true integrity. She is the real champion today."

Most of us would go into a rant if that kind of unfairness happened to us. But while Wendy doesn't think the rule stands out as the most judicious standard in the book, she was not about to lose her cool about it. "Did I think this rule was fair, considering I didn't even touch the ball? Absolutely not! But a rule is a rule, so I called the penalty."

Then she continued to explain her motive for giving herself an added stroke when a lesser person would have waved it off with a shrug.

"Just like God calls us to obey His commands, I am called to adhere to the rules of golf. I also believed that God would reward me later for my integrity and my honesty. No one but me saw the ball move—not Juli, not even the TV camera. But I knew it moved, and that was all that mattered."

It mattered to Wendy because she plays golf for more than the money. As a strong Christian and a regular participant in a Bible study that is conducted for golfers on the LPGA Tour, Ward understood that her actions go beyond how they affect her personally. She "gets it" that Christian athletes answer to a higher, more respectable standard.

"I guess it was what Jesus would have done, and I was wearing one of those WWJD bracelets."

In John 14, Jesus told us that He is the way, the truth, and the life. And because He is the truth—because He is truth personified—He leads the way for us at any time we might wonder if truth, integrity, and honesty are as important as whatever personal goals we might be able to achieve without them.

Wendy knows truth because she knows Jesus.

"I was disappointed to have lost a major championship, but I felt as if I did the right thing in God's eyes, and that is more important to me," she said later as she looked back on that odd occurrence on the thirteenth green. She chose the more important way, and she has gained more from that decision than the extra money could ever have brought her if she had won it while knowing that she had not won it honestly.

Looking Up

Nobody was looking.

That is a perfect situation in which to find ourselves when we want to do something that we know is not right. Whether it is Wendy Ward on the golf course or a married couple named Ananias and Sapphira, the opportunity presented by secrecy can be a huge threat to integrity. We know what Wendy did. But what about Ananias and Sapphira?

This couple had completed a business transaction. They owned some land, and they decided that it was time to sell it. After they found a buyer and made the transaction, they decided to give some of the money to the church.

As they prepared to donate the money, they talked with each other about how much to give. "With his wife's full knowledge," Acts 5:2 reports, "he kept back part of the money for himself."

With the rest of the money, Ananias presented an offering to the Lord, laying it at the feet of the apostle.

Sounds like a pretty good thing to do, doesn't it?

But there was a problem. In the way they presented the money, they left the impression with the recipients of the money that they had given it all (this came clear when Sapphira answered Peter's questions in verse 8). When they thought no one was looking, they conspired to deceive.

There is a principle at work here that affects us all. "Do not be deceived: God cannot be mocked" (Galatians 6:7). We cannot hide anything from Him.

Today, occasions will arise when we look around to see if anyone is looking. When we do, we have to make sure we look up.

The Bible Addresses Integrity

"Then the Lord said to Satan, 'Have you considered my servant Job? There is no one on earth like him; he is blameless and upright, a man who fears God and shuns evil. And he still maintains his integrity, though you incited me against him to ruin him without any reason.'" (Job 2:3)

"Lord, who may dwell in your sanctuary? Who may live on

your holy hill? He whose walk is blameless and who does what is righteous, who speaks the truth from his heart." (Psalm 15:1–2)

"The integrity of the upright guides them, but the unfaithful are destroyed by their duplicity." (Proverbs 11:3)

"A truthful witness gives honest testimony." (Proverbs 12:17)

"Do not lie to each other, since you have taken off your old self with its practices and have put on the new self." (Colossians 3:9–10)

Darrell Waltrip

True Love

Husbands, love your wives, just as Christ loved the church.
—Ephesians 5:25

DARRELL WALTRIP IS ONE OF THE GOODEST of
the good old boys. He's been around stock car driving for so long he probably has a hard time making right turns. Well respected as a driver, his popularity blew up when he handed in his helmet and picked up a microphone
as a NASCAR TV analyst. He became the beloved boogity man—known
for his trademark "boogity, boogity, boogity" shout-out to the drivers as
they cross the starting line to begin their noisy quest toward another check-
ered flag.

But if all you think Darrell Waltrip stands for is a successful career as a
driver and as a talker on NASCAR telecasts, your knowledge of the man
from Owensboro, Kentucky, needs a serious overhaul. No, this man's life
didn't hit full throttle until a woman named Stevie got his attention.

Let's go back a couple of decades and look at who Darrell Waltrip used
to be. In 1983, if ol' DW had been called on to be on television as a color
commentator, his ratings would have been XFL-like. Let's just say that he
was not a well-liked driver in those days.

Here's how he describes the 1983 DW. "I had just come off two great
years as a driver. I'd won twelve races each of those two years. I won the
driving championship both years, and I was really feeling quite invincible. I
had the world by the tail, and nobody could tell me anything. I was pretty
arrogant, pretty cocky, pretty much an 'I' person. I was having great success
in my career but having a lot of failures otherwise."

Enter Stevie. Not literally, actually—she and Darrell had been married
for thirteen years already. But Stevie is one smart woman, and she knew him
well enough to know that he needed to change. And she loved him enough
to fire a little tough love his way.

"She knew that we were on a path of destruction," Waltrip recalls, "and
she started pressing me to get my priorities straight and to stop worrying
about my career and making money."

Love is funny that way. Here was a guy who had made it to the top of

16

his profession—a guy whose sometimes-surly attitude made it difficult for most people to get close to him, let alone tell him what to do. But the person who loved him the most was not about to let him throw everything away. Risking rejection and perhaps a backlash of anger, she laid it on the line for her husband.

And Darrell, because of his reciprocal love for Stevie, followed her wise advice. She helped move him back toward his roots—his roots in the church.

Darrell was no stranger to the church. His parents were Christians, his dad was a deacon, and the Waltrip clan was an "every time the church door is open" kind of family. He knew about the gospel of Jesus Christ and its effect on his life.

Yet like so many athletes who get caught up in the drive for success, Darrell had let racing take him away from those roots. The best move he ever made was to let Stevie bring him back.

Stevie and Darrell began attending a Wednesday night Bible study led by Dr. Cortez Cooper, who knew Darrell well enough to know that he would have to love this renegade of a stock car driver back to Jesus. Waltrip recalls him as "the first minister in my whole life who could really make the Bible come alive."

Not long after Stevie threw down the gauntlet, Darrell took Dr. Cooper's messages to heart and "made a commitment to Jesus Christ," as he describes it. "We prayed that the Lord would help me get my priorities and my life straightened out. I made a commitment to the Lord [in 1983] and have been trying hard to live up to it ever since."

That may be the spiritual highlight for the Darrell and Stevie Waltrip Love Story, but it's certainly not the only one.

Another crisis that would lead to indescribable joy for the couple relates to children.

For the first several years of their marriage, the Waltrips had no children. But it wasn't because they didn't want them. They worked with doctors, hoping that Stevie could get pregnant. For seven years, they hoped and prayed for a child. Finally, a child was conceived. But before the baby was born, Stevie suffered a miscarriage. Then it happened again.

Both of them say that was the toughest thing they have had to face, and who can doubt that? They were in their mid-thirties, and God seemed to be closing the door on their having children.

But they didn't give up, and in 1989—after they had been married nineteen years—Jessica was born. Three years later, Sarah was welcomed into the Waltrip household. True love and a ton of patience had won out.

When Waltrip considers the difficulties he and Stevie endured to have those children, he feels their arrival coincided with a further maturity in his life. "I believe that the Lord didn't want me to have children at first. I think He withheld children from me . . . because I wouldn't have made a good father back in those early days. I really think the Lord held the kids back until a time when I could really appreciate children."

For her part, Stevie sees the love Darrell has grown into—the love that seemed so foreign before but is so natural now. "Since he became a father, he's gentler and more thoughtful. He has chosen to be a good husband and a good father. Love is a choice. You choose whether you want to stay married. You have to work at it."

Looking Up

Submit and love.

Okay, the love thing probably doesn't seem to be a problem. Everybody wants to love and be loved—whether they admit it or not.

But submit? Are you kidding me?

If you are looking ahead at marriage someday, and you are a young lady, the idea of submitting just might sound a little like a coach telling you to do twenty more laps around the gym. You know it might be good for you, but you sure don't want to do it.

First, let's look at love. It's what the guy is told to do. Husbands, it seems, don't always understand that the commitment to cherish and love are essential to a wife's well-being. Therefore, Paul had to spell it out. After all, a man may look at Ephesians 5:25 and wonder, "What's the deal? I told her I loved her when we got married. Isn't that enough?"

Well, no. Love is a continual thing, and it takes work.

Then there's that submission thing. Paul said, "Submit to your husbands as to the Lord. For the husband is the head of the wife as Christ is the head of the church." Here's how it's supposed to work:

- A guy will treat his wife with the same love, devotion, care, and concern that Christ uses in working with the church—even to the point of total and complete sacrifice.
- If he does, then his wife will respond with a respectful submission.

A guy has to remember this: Jesus said in Matthew 20:28 that He "did not come to be served, but to serve." Men are not here to be served by their wives, but to serve them.

With Stevie and Darrell Waltrip, things didn't get going properly in the love department until Stevie used her wisdom as a strong Christian to influence Darrell to get his relationship with God straightened out. When he did, then he could serve, which freed Stevie to respond properly to him.

Are you in love? Or thinking about it in the not-too-distant future? Make sure your love is controlled first by a proper love relationship with God and His standards. Then get that submission and love idea down.

That's how God is glorified, and that's how a marriage gets on the fast track to success.

The Bible Addresses Love and Marriage

"He who finds a good wife finds what is good and receives favor from the Lord." (Proverbs 18:22)

"A man will leave his father and mother and be united to his wife, and they will become one flesh." (Genesis 2:24)

"A wife of noble character is her husband's crown." (Proverbs 12:4)

"Husbands, in the same way be considerate as you live with your wives, and treat them with respect as the weaker partner and as heirs with you of the gracious gift of life, so that nothing will hinder your prayers." (1 Peter 3:7)

David Robinson
Big Guy, Big Heart

A generous man will himself be blessed, for he shares his food with the poor.
—Proverbs 22:9

WHAT DAVID ROBINSON IS TRYING TO DO IN San Antonio, Texas, after he retired from basketball is probably a lot harder than what he did before he retired.

As a basketball player, all he had to do was score about 20 points in 48 minutes of NBA hoops, grab about 10 rebounds, block a couple of shots, and help his team win two NBA titles. It took a lot of running up and down the court, a good deal of jumping, and a lot of leadership. It took putting up with writers who couldn't wait to color him soft if his team faltered, simply because the man had put his faith in Jesus Christ. And it took a lot of pain, for Robinson often had to endure a back that hurt like crazy.

For more than a decade, David Robinson did the task of excelling in the NBA, and he did it well. One year he was named Most Valuable Player in the entire league. He was a ten-time All-Star and three-time Olympian. *Sports Illustrated* bestowed on him its most prestigious award in 2003: Sportsman of the Year.

For a guy that big, it was a lot of work to haul up and down the court all those years and rack up all the awards and rings he did. And for his efforts, the San Antonio Spurs gladly paid him tens of millions of dollars to bring fame and TV cameras to their city.

Then, in 2003, after 34,271 minutes of NBA action, he took off his big number 50 jersey for the last time and traded it in for a suit and tie.

Mr. Robinson was going back to school. Not as a student this time, though. That stint was completed once he was done as a midshipman at the Naval Academy.

Now David Robinson was going to pour himself more completely into an educational adventure that would take lots of his money and lots of his time. And much of his heart.

While many retired NBA players head for the beach or the broadcast booth, Robinson headed for the books. He and his wife, Valerie, used $9 million of their own money to build a new school in San Antonio, a school for kids who needed a hand up. Nine million dollars, no matter what a guy made playing basketball, is a boatload of presidents. It is, in fact, considered to be the largest contribution ever made by a professional athlete.

The Carver Academy, located in a part of San Antonio that is populated by poorer minority families, is a private, nondenominational Christian school where kids are given a true chance to succeed. Named after the great African-American scientist, philosopher, and Christian, George Washington Carver, the school has set out to make a difference in the Alamo city. According to Robinson, "It is our hope that The Carver Academy will spark the hunger to serve in our children and provide an oasis of learning for parents and the community."

Robinson did not simply write a big check for The Carver Academy and then jet out of San Antonio for Hawaii. He is a hands-on part of what is going on at the school. "It's important for me to be there to inspire and encourage people," he told *Christianity Today* magazine. "You can't really motivate kids unless you foster a loving, nurturing atmosphere. I want kids to feel that they belong to something special."

He is passionate about the success of the kids who call Carver theirs. Because he was not trained in educational administration, he leaves the day-to-day school operations up to those who are; but he's not in the teacher's lounge telling old basketball stories.

Robinson is the chairman of the board of the school, which gives him a voice in the future of the academic endeavor. In addition, Robinson is hard at work doing something that to many would be harder than scoring the 73 points he once put up in an NBA game. He is trying to raise $30 million as an endowment for the school. He also speaks in chapel, and when he does, he tells students about biblical heroes who have, as he says, "laid the foundation" of the faith.

Generosity was not a late addition to Robinson's résumé. Throughout his outstanding NBA sojourn, he regularly gave 10 percent of his salary to support the David Robinson Foundation, an organization that allowed him early on to support young people and provide hope for those with disadvantages. When he and Valerie began the foundation, they chose as their theme Bible verse Matthew 5:14, which says, "You are the light of the world. A city set on a hill cannot be hidden." And neither can a man who stands seven foot one. Robinson stands tall and properly conspicuous as a generous man.

Through the foundation and a couple of its programs, Valerie and David have helped needy infants through the Ruth Project and hungry citizens through another outreach called Feed My Sheep.

And before The Carver Academy had grown to what it is today, there was the promise Robinson made to ninety-five fifth-grade students at an elementary school in San Antonio. "Finish high school," he told them, "and I'll give you two thousand dollars toward college." In 1998, fifty of those kids earned the scholarships.

Robinson stands amazed at what God has enabled him to do. He understands that his talent and his height (which took him from six foot four to seven foot one while he was at the Naval Academy) are gifts from God. And what is he to do but help others with this gift.

"It is amazing to me that God has entrusted me with this," he says.

And San Antonio is amazed at what David Robinson has done with that trust.

Looking Up

Paul sounds pretty excited in his second letter to the Corinthians when he writes to the people about their generosity. He talked about their "eagerness to help," their "enthusiasm" about giving, and their "generous gift." The people of Corinth had obviously been moved by their faith life to give back to God of the money they had been entrusted with.

A bunch of high school kids saw a need in a Caribbean country—a need for a small Christian school to have a playground for its kids. So they got together with the help of some adults and planned a trip. One of the key efforts, of course, was to raise the needed $20,000 for the expenses—including the cost of the playground equipment. The teens were willing and eager to give of their summer vacation and their hard work in the hot sun to get this job done. But one stepped up and showed true generosity. One student decided to donate every dollar in a bank account that had been accumulating for years. It was being saved up to buy a car—something every teen wants. But for the kids of this school, this teenager gave it all.

That is the enthusiasm Paul was talking about. That is the generosity David Robinson demonstrates.

Our challenge is to be somewhere in the middle. Perhaps we can't give it all as this teen did. Perhaps we can't start a major project as Robinson did. But we can all have an "eagerness to help." We can all give with "enthusiasm."

Giving is one of the important sacrifices of the Christian faith. Paul said, "Whoever sows sparingly will also reap sparingly" (2 Corinthians 9:6). It's like this. That harvest is a spiritual one. One of the key ways to be rich toward God and to enhance our relationship with Him is through our generosity to others—as a worshipful sacrifice to Him.

The Bible Addresses Generosity

"Good will come to him who is generous and lends freely, who conducts his affairs with justice." (Psalm 112:5)

"Blessed is the man who has regard for the weak; the Lord delivers him in times of trouble." (Psalm 41:1)

"We have different gifts, according to the grace given us. . . . If it is contributing to the needs of others, let him give generously." (Romans 12:6–7)

4

Laura Wilkinson

Grace for All Seasons

Each one should use whatever gift he has received to serve others,
faithfully administering God's grace in its various forms.
—1 Peter 4:10

ONE OF THE THINGS THAT MOST SURPRISED
people about Laura Wilkinson when she won the gold medal in the 2000
Olympics turned out to be the very thing that made her such a compelling
figure four years later.

In 2000, Wilkinson shocked the world of Olympic diving by coming
absolutely out of nowhere to capture the gold medal in platform diving.
Seeing this relatively unknown diver beat back the more established and
more highly favored Chinese divers was a treat for American fans who didn't
think the red, white, and blue had a chance.

You only have to look at the names of the winners in the previous eight
Olympics to know that a name like Wilkinson was not expected to be atop
the standings in platform diving. In 1968, Milena Duchková, Czechoslo-
vakia; 1972, Ulrika Knape, Sweden; 1976, Elena Vaytsekhovskaya, USSR;
1980, Marina Jäschke, East Germany; 1984, Zhou Jihong, China; 1988, Xu
Yanmei, China; 1992 and 1996, Fu Mingxia, China.

So what was a girl from Houston, Texas, doing adding her name to that
list? How did Laura Wilkinson become the first American since 1964 to
stand atop the podium after platform diving was done? And what surprise
did she have for many interested Americans?

Just six months before the athletes convened in Sydney, Australia, Wilkinson's chances of winning a gold medal in the 2000 Olympics were about
as low as they could go. While competing in a diving meet, Laura broke her
foot. She faced a choice—either she could have surgery and forgo a trip to
Sydney or she could hobble her way through the next few weeks and give it
her best shot Down Under. She opted to go for it.

So there she was, wearing a kayak shoe on her broken foot when she
climbed the stairs to the top of the ten-meter platform. There she would
discard the shoe and look out over the crowd, searching for friendly faces—
then take off for the water.

Everyone who knew anything about diving knew that Laura was a phenomenal diver. She was, after all, a nine-time U.S. National diving champion.

But because of her injury and because of the perceived dominance of the Chinese divers, no one was much surprised when she found herself in eighth place after the first of five dives. Wilkinson was determined to come back, though. The smile on her face and her calm demeanor might have been misread by some who didn't know her resolve, but she had a strength that she claimed as hers before every dive.

By the time she was on the platform for her third dive, she was within striking distance of the Chinese divers and first place. She took off from the platform for her reverse two-and-a-half somersault with a tuck. She entered the water with the slightest of splashes—always a thrill for those who watch and always a good sign for the judges. When she emerged from the water, Laura Wilkinson was in first place.

Her fourth dive was an inward two-and-a-half somersault from the pike position, a dive that often gave her trouble. She retained her lead with that dive, leaving her with one more to go. Gold would be hers if she could nail it.

As she and her kayak-shoe-clad broken foot climbed the ladder, Laura recited Philippians 4:13, "I can do all things through him who gives me strength." She tossed the shoe aside, gathered her thoughts, and dived right into the history books. Gold was hers.

Laura Wilkinson became both an Olympic hero and a role model for Christians everywhere for her courage and her solid faith. She proudly stood and accepted her medal as a chest-thumping country watched.

That was 2000. In 2004, Wilkinson was tested again. And again, she came through. This time, however, it wasn't gold that she displayed proudly at the end of the platform diving competition. It was grace.

Pure, unadulterated Christian grace. Poise under fire. Love under duress. Grace in the most pressure-packed circumstances.

This time there would be no come-from-behind victory.

She found herself trailing again—similar to her position in 2000. When a couple of divers in front of her made major errors, it appeared that it might be déjà vu all over again. Yet when Wilkinson flew off the platform this time, she didn't quite get it right. If you must know—and often most of us have no idea that these things have happened to divers—she had miscalculated the release of her tuck position. That error, perhaps unseen by those watching at home, left her in fifth place.

Yet those who were really paying attention saw something that's maybe even better than back-to-back golds. Laura Wilkinson could be seen smiling, congratulating other divers, handing out towels, and helping others despite her own disappointments.

The smile that won people's hearts when she captured the gold was still there. It was a smile that came from true joy—joy of having Jesus as her Savior whether she had won gold or belly-flopped into the Olympic pool. And that joy enabled her to demonstrate unselfish love and grace to everyone who observed her.

It was not gold that made Laura Wilkinson the remarkable person she is. It was grace. God's grace.

Looking Up

Sometimes it takes no more than three seconds to see how hard it is for some people to demonstrate grace.

Try sitting at a traffic light for three seconds after the light turns green. Grace does not describe what the guy behind you with his hand on the horn is showing.

Try not moving up for three seconds when the ticket line finally moves outside the movie theater. The biker guy behind you sighing heavily does not have grace on his mind.

In a world in which everyone seems to be going at breakneck speed to who knows where, it's often hard to see much grace being manifested.

For that reason, we who have Jesus in our hearts have a wide-open door that can lead to testifying of God's love. Imagine what it does to others in a hostile world when we speak politely, hold doors open, pick up dropped items, talk kindly on the phone, and smile hello to the girl running the cash register at Wal-Mart.

Paul called for us to have conversations that are full of grace (Colossians 4:6). James reminds us that grace comes from God (4:6). And Peter reminds us that we are to grow in grace (2 Peter 3:18).

Just as Laura set aside her disappointment and graced competitors with love and goodness, so we can set aside what troubles us and bestow a bit of the grace God gives us on others.

It'll make them and Him smile approval on our actions.

The Bible Addresses Grace

"God is able to make all grace abound to you, so that in all things at all times, having all that you need, you will abound in every good work." (2 Corinthians 9:8)

"I always thank God for you because of his grace given you in Christ Jesus." (1 Corinthians 1:4)

"Let your conversation be always full of grace." (Colossians 4:6)

5

Shaun Alexander

Kids' Stuff

Blessed is he who is kind to the needy.
—*Proverbs 14:21*
See that you do not look down on one of these little ones.
—*Matthew 18:10*

PEOPLE ALWAYS SEEM TO BE CHASING Shaun
Alexander. Linebackers. Defensive linemen. Safeties. Reporters.

Most times someone eventually catches him, but through the first six years of his NFL career, he got away from tacklers enough to gain more than 7,800 yards and score 89 touchdowns. And he probably even missed out on a couple of interviews.

But when it comes to running and chasing, Shaun Alexander has his own plan. It is one that he shares with the "little brothers," as he calls the kids he tries to help through the Shaun Alexander Foundation. What he says they are up to is "chasing God."

When Alexander started the foundation in 2001, he did so because, as he puts it, "I play to make a difference in their lives. It's not just about football. It's about helping others."

Specifically, Alexander has set out to help boys—boys who through no fault of their own are forced to grow up without the proper modeling at home. Alexander's organization points out that this is a "plague haunting millions of children in the United States" and that "40 percent of the children in the United States do not live with their father."

Alexander understands that young men are most affected by this cultural phenomenon. He notes that "fatherless children are twice as likely to drop out of school and twice as likely to be jailed." Unless they get some help. Unless somebody reaches out to empower them to overcome their disadvantages. Unless Shaun Alexander helps.

"A lot of people around me are asking me why I'm doing this," the 2005 NFL Most Valuable Player says. "They're telling me I shouldn't be doing this, but you know what? You can't out-give God. It's all about giving back."

The powerful running back, who made his first appearance in the Super

Bowl on February 5, 2006, when the Seattle Seahawks took on the Pittsburgh Steelers in Detroit, knows about growing up without a father in the home. It happened to him and his brother, Durran.

Shaun Alexander grew up in Florence, Kentucky, a city that lies a few miles south of the Ohio River and down I–75 a piece from Cincinnati. It's a town that is most famous for the Florence Mall that has the iconoclastic "Florence Y'all" water tower, and Florence is the address for the Cincinnati International Airport.

Assume no affront to Shaun's mom, Carol, when her son talks about helping kids without a dad. He knows that Mom did a great job of guiding him and Durran. One went to the University of Alabama—the other, Notre Dame. One played football, the other played in the band. Carol's kids did quite well, thank you.

She taught her boys how to battle. She fought colon cancer when Shaun was in high school. She beat it when he and Durran were in college.

After the boys were done with college, she went back to school and picked up a degree in mental health and human services from Northern Kentucky University in 2001. Now she works for the same school district where her boys went to school. She works to prevent kids from being truant, and she helps young parents improve their parenting ability.

She did such a marvelous job of raising her boys after her husband left her when they were little, that Shaun had to go all the way to Tuscaloosa, Alabama, to find out that he was poor. Despite the fact that the three of them lived in a two-bedroom apartment, Shaun thought they were doing fine because his mom was always helping others. *We must be okay,* he figured, *if Mom's doing stuff for everybody else.*

One way Shaun is helping the kids of Florence is by giving them a place to go to swim and play ball. When he was a kid, Shaun didn't have the money to go to the YMCA. So when he struck it rich in the NFL, he bought it. Now the Alexander Family Community Center will open its doors to kids like Shaun.

Shaun Alexander has never forgotten Florence. In fact, the Shaun Alexander Foundation is based in Florence, and Durran runs it. The football-playing brother keeps returning to Florence, where he visits kids in the schools. He also calls the Florence High School football team's coaching staff before game time on Friday nights—just to let them know he's thinking of them.

Florence is where Shaun was when he trusted Jesus Christ as Savior, which gives him further incentive to provide direction for today's generation of kids in his hometown.

Growing up in Florence, he had no designs on being a big football star. He still claims that while the neighborhood kids wanted to go over to the vacant lot and play tackle football or baseball, he wanted to find a vacant couch and read.

And when he got talked into playing football in high school and developed into one of the best players in the United States, he still didn't think of himself as special. Finally, though, he found a way to make it all seem okay. The smiling, fun-loving kid simply had "a gift from God." He had been given the gift to "play football better than a lot of people."

Once he decided it was okay to be pretty good (since that's the way God designed him), he was driven to use that gift. He was challenged to keep getting better. He began to chase greatness. And once he established himself, he began to chase kids he could help. Kids like Alex.

Teenager. Crohn's disease. Alex went to an NFL game in Seattle and got to meet Shaun. They became buddies. They swapped Bible verses. Alex started a foundation with Shaun's help. Shaun played in his golf tournament. Alex says Shaun helps him when things get tough. And Shaun, well, you know how those stories go. Alex helps Shaun keep going as well.

That's the way it is with kids' stuff, done in Jesus' name.

Looking Up

Imagine doing something that you know beyond a doubt is God's work. Imagine how rewarding it would be.

We don't have to imagine it.

We can do it.

Let's examine one thing that God asks us to do, and as we do, we'll see why it is so important to Him.

In Galatians 6:10, the apostle Paul said this: "Therefore, as we have opportunity, let us do good to all people, especially to those who belong to the family of believers." This leaves no doubt. We must look for ways to help others—both in and out of the family of God. One specific way is found in James 1:27, where we are told to look after "orphans and widows."

Why does God take a special interest in orphans? That answer is found in Psalm 68:5, which tells us that "God is the father to the fatherless." Clearly, God longs to see those without a human father cared for, and just as clearly, He expects us to help out in taking care of them.

Psalm 82:3–4 says, "Defend the cause of the weak and fatherless; maintain the rights of the poor and oppressed. Rescue the weak and needy."

Sometimes we think we need to turn over such grand acts of kindness to the Shaun Alexanders of the world. After all, S. A. is the one with all the money.

That, however, is not the point. Unlike most athletes at contract time, it's not about the money. It's about the effort. It's about the love. It's about the compassion.

Just as Shaun Alexander returned to Florence to help the kids in his old neighborhood as a way of giving back for all that God has given him, we too need to find a place to take our compassion. We too need to do something that we know beyond doubt is God's work.

Please the Father. Reach out to the fatherless. Help the weak.

The Bible Addresses Reaching Out to the Needy

"Blessed is he who has regard for the weak; the Lord delivers him in times of trouble." (Psalm 41:1)

"[A wife of noble character] opens her arms to the poor and extends her hands to the needy." (Proverbs 31:20)

"Share your food with the hungry and . . . provide the poor wanderer with shelter." (Isaiah 58:7)

6

Michael Redd
Like Father, Like Son

The father of a righteous man has great joy;
he who has a wise son delights in him.
—*Proverbs 23:24*

IN COLUMBUS, OHIO, RED IS A COLOR THAT gets a lot of respect. Red as in scarlet, half of the main colors of the Ohio State Buckeyes.

But in recent years, Redd has been getting a lot attention in the respect category as well. Redd as in Michael, the pro basketball player, and James, the local pastor.

This is the story of two members of one family who can teach us all something about the value of relationship—the importance of a father and a son sticking together.

Michael Redd is the more famous basketball player of the two, but James was a pretty good player in his own right. One generation ago, James was an All-Star hoopster at Columbus West High School in the Buckeye state capital. He gained national attention as a guard—attracting the longing gaze of men like Bob Knight, George Raveling, and even Dick Vitale in his day as a college coach.

James, showing his true character even as a teenager, swept aside all of those glitzy offers to play big-time basketball. His mom was sick, and he knew she needed him. Not wanting to be too far away from her or too distracted from helping her, he stayed nearby and went to Capital University in Columbus.

That's where he met his wife, Haji—which to James Redd is a pretty clear indication that he had done the right thing by going to Capital.

A few years later, along came Michael, who would eventually be better than his dad at hoops, and bigger—which meant that after *his* nationally acclaimed high school career ended at Columbus West, when he stayed home to play college ball, it was not going to be at Division III Capital. It was going to be at Ohio State University. Redd. Scarlet. It's all working out.

Before Michael matriculated at the biggest university in the Big Ten, he and his dad shared a dream. James never made it big in hoops or struck it rich in any way other than spiritual and familial. His heart was dedicated to serving God as a pastor, so after working for Pepsi during the week, he became Pastor James on the weekend.

These were small churches. Storefront churches. Basement churches. Struggling to get enough people but dedicated to preaching the Word of God and spreading the gospel of Jesus.

Michael saw his father's dilemma, even as a high school senior at West. And just as James Redd had decided to do something to help his mother in need, Michael decided that he wanted to do something to help his dad in ministry.

But this wasn't about staying home and going to a small college to remain near the family. This was about going to Ohio State as a stepping-stone to the true big-time in basketball—the NBA. As a senior in high school, Michael told his dad that if he made it to the show, he would buy him a church.

A church.

Dads hear their sons share a lot of dreams. Some kids tell their dads they're going to become doctors. Others tell their dads they're setting out to become president. How many tell their dad, "I'm going to buy you a church"?

So off Michael went to Ohio State. In his first year, he led Big Ten freshmen in scoring. It was no secret that this Redd could light 'em up. With his size, speed, and shooting prowess, the NBA looked like a better target every season.

By the time Redd completed his junior year at OSU, he decided he was ready. The time was coming, it seemed, when he might be able to follow through on his promise.

But NBA executives had their doubts about the left-handed sharp-shooter. On draft day, Michael and his family had to sit through forty-two excruciating selections until he was picked by the Milwaukee Bucks.

Perhaps Michael Redd would have to face some difficult realities about his dreams—about both the NBA and bricks and mortar for Dad. The forty-third best player in the country is not going to get much NBA playing time. And although his first-year money of $300,000 was a lot, it's hardly enough to live on and still purchase a church building.

So Redd worked hard. He practiced diligently. He was a model citizen for the Bucks.

So what happened in season one?

Michael played a grand total of thirty-five minutes. The whole season. He got to report in to a measly six games in 2000–2001. He scored 13 points. Yet he earned the respect of his teammates with hard work. "Not only was he making himself better, but he was also pushing his teammates to make them better," says Joel Pryzbilla of Redd's first year. "He always kept his head up."

There was a dream pushing him forward—not only to be a good NBA player but also to be able to buy his dad that church building.

In his sophomore season at Milwaukee, he averaged 11 points a game. In 2002–2003, he was at 15 points per game. And then came 2004–2005, when he emerged as one of the best guards in the league. He averaged 21.7 points a game in his fourth year and increased that to 23 a game the following season.

Now he was ready. Now Michael Redd, who used to tell his father, "O ye of little faith," when his dad doubted that his son could deliver on his dream, was ready. In 2005, he inked a huge multi-million-dollar deal.

When 2006 began, the Philadelphia Deliverance Church of Christ had a beautiful new home. It sits in the eastern part of Columbus, a gleaming reminder of a boy's love for his dad. And it has enabled Rev. James Redd to have a true church home for his flock.

What had been home to about twenty-five of the faithful now opens its doors to more than three hundred people on a Sunday. Sometimes, when he can, Michael Redd helps his father with the worship service by playing the drums. And someday, Michael says, he may even want to take over for his dad as the pastor of the church.

"I consider my dad one of the greatest pastors in the world," Michael says of the man who taught him how to play basketball—and how to give.

If you're going to give a man a church, it's probably a good idea to give it to a man you know better than anyone else, and whom you still think is the best there is.

These are two men who truly know how to give.

Looking Up

There is perhaps no better picture of a son giving back to his father—and the father receiving that gift with such joy—as the story of Joseph and his father Jacob.

Joseph not only received the gift of grain and sustenance from his son because of his position as a leader in Egypt, he also received his son back. For years, Jacob thought Joseph was dead—attacked by a wild animal as Joseph's brothers had told him.

But then came the news that Joseph was in Egypt and he was in charge.

Imagine the celebration when they got together for the first time. Don't imagine it, read about it.

"Joseph had his chariot made ready and went to Goshen to meet his father Israel [Jacob]. As soon as Joseph appeared before him, he threw his arms around his father and wept for a long time. Israel said to Joseph, 'Now I am ready to die, since I have seen for myself that you are alive.'" (Genesis 46:29–30). The old man's life was fulfilled with the gift of knowing that Joseph was still alive.

Fathers. Sons. What a special and unique relationship.

How dads and their sons interact—especially for those who know Jesus and want to serve God—should mirror as much as possible the relationship between the heavenly Father and His only Son.

Jesus came to earth to do God's bidding, and before He returned to the Father, He gave a great gift, himself, to fulfill God's plan for the earth.

When dads and their sons have a relationship of mutual love and care, they point God-ward to all who see them.

The Bible Addresses Fathers and Sons

"My son, do not forget my teaching, but keep my commands in your heart." (Proverbs 3:1)

"The righteous man leads a blameless life; blessed are his children after him." (Proverbs 20:7)

7

Kevin Mawae
God's Care
Good and upright is the Lord.
—Psalm 25:8

RAISED IN A MILITARY FAMILY, KEVIN MAWAE had to get used to losing friends. The Mawae family would often have to relocate when Kevin's dad was reassigned to a new location. When that happened, "you dumped your friends," as he describes it—and then you moved on to find new ones.

In a family so transient, what came in handy for Kevin was having a special sibling. John and Kevin Mawae were extremely close. Only a year separated them, and the continual movement and changes brought them even closer.

When they went away to college at Louisiana State University, they kept close—they were roommates.

On the football field at LSU, they went up against each other in practice, John as a nose tackle and Kevin as center. John, being older, didn't want Kevin to get the upper hand, so when they battled on the field, they went hard. It was a civil war on the practice field. But through it all, they remained close.

After college, Kevin moved on to the NFL, playing first for the Seattle Seahawks. In 1996, while he was in his third year with the Seahawks, something happened that would profoundly alter Kevin's life.

John, who had built up a reputation as something of a partier, turned his life around. He had become a changed person.

Something was different about John, and he was eager to get together with Kevin and tell him about it.

But he never got that chance.

John and a friend were traveling home from New Orleans. His friend, who was driving, fell asleep at the wheel. His vehicle crashed into a cement truck that was parked beside the road. John was killed instantly.

What was Kevin to do? How would he handle losing his best friend—his close companion for twenty-five years?

"You can go two ways with something like this," Mawae says in reflection of his feelings at the time. "You can go totally bad, or you can go the other way and dedicate yourself and what you do to John's memory."

Kevin decided to take the second path.

The first thing he did was try to figure out what happened with John before the accident. Why had he changed, and what was it he wanted to share with Kevin about his new life?

Part of the answer, he discovered, could be found in a huge event that was about to take place in John's life. He was engaged, and to honor his future wife, he was taking confirmation classes at her church. "It was during this time of going through the course that his demeanor changed," Kevin recalls. "He began contacting people from his past, asking forgiveness for some of the things he had done."

He wanted to talk to Kevin as well. "The night before the accident," Kevin recalls, "I spoke with him on the phone. He said he needed to talk to me about something—that he would call me the next day."

But the next call he got was not from John. It was from another brother, and he had bad news. John was gone.

They would never share that special phone call in which John would tell Kevin about his new direction in life.

It's difficult to turn from a life-altering event such as a tragic, unexpected death and say, "Wow, God! You really love me." It's difficult to peer through the pain and see anything good.

But God has a way of breaking through the fog.

For Kevin, it was good news in his own life that helped alter his thinking.

"I didn't sense God's care in my life until a few months later. After John's death, I was pretty torn," he says. And anyone who has experienced tragedy understands.

"Two months after his death, my wife became pregnant. This is when the questions about who God is really began. I questioned God's ability to give and then take—the miracle of birth, how I lost my closest friend but was about to have a child of my own."

Where could he look for answers? Knowing that somehow the change in his brother had been spiritual, the younger Mawae began searching the Bible for answers. "I began going to Bible studies and reading the Bible, searching for answers. It was then that I felt God begin His work in me.

"I finally came to the realization that God *is* in control and always had been.

"Eventually, I gave my life to Christ, including my despair, questions, and disbelief. On June 17, 1997, I got saved."

He found what John had found, he believes. "I believe he found the Truth, and this caused his changed demeanor. God used John's death to bring me and my family to Christ."

Tragedy can change people. And even though Kevin found eternal life through searching the Bible to see what had changed John's life, he still had to deal with the great loss in his life. For many, such a circumstance can lead them to push away from God—to be angry with His dealings that cause so much pain.

Mawae, however, took a different route.

"I think that what kept me from getting bitter about John's death was the sweet joy of knowing that I was to become a father myself. I had just lost someone so dear to me, but it's like God was replacing my brother with the birth of my son, Kirkland.

"It could have happened only in God's timing."

Kevin also sensed God's care in giving him a new cadre of friends. "I was surrounded by friends who were all believers. Todd and Susan Peterson. Grant and Emily Williams. Howard Ballard. Ronnie and Kris Harris. Barb and Chuck Snyder, who led the Seattle Seahawks' Bible study. They became a support system who, instead of making excuses and lame sympathies, helped me to understand that God's will always prevails."

Kevin realizes that what John had in his newfound faith and what he gained through his search for truth has provided peace that he did not have before. He has the comfort of knowing that his faith has given him a new purpose and drive in life.

"God has placed me here to use my position to reach out to people who otherwise wouldn't be around a professional athlete," says Mawae. "I have the ability to reach out and touch people through my experiences. I can use my testimony to influence people's lives."

Mawae now has peace in knowing that his brother is experiencing the gift of eternal life, promised to those who acknowledge Jesus Christ as their

Lord and Savior. And since that day when Kevin called on the name of the Lord, he has experienced some great changes in his life too. The New York Jets signed him to a free-agent contract in 1999 that made him the highest-paid center in the history of the NFL, and he has made five consecutive trips to the prestigious Pro Bowl since.

Mawae's life is now far more than football. Through tragedy, he has received something all the world's wealth and fame couldn't provide: peace and joy through a relationship with Jesus Christ.

"It turned my life around," says Mawae.

God's care has taken a bereaved brother and turned him into a shining beacon of hope for others.

Looking Up

Death. Tragedy. Loss.

It can make us or it can break us. It all depends on how we view God.

If we think of God as a cold, calculating being who does not care for us, then we will respond in anger in bad times. We will turn our back on Him and reject all of the promises that tell us that He cares.

If we think of God as a loving yet sometimes mysterious Father whose heart breaks when ours does, then we can find hope in the midst of terrible circumstances.

Turning tragedy into glory is not easy. Yet think of what happened to Kevin Mawae. Suppose that although John had trusted Christ and had his eternal reservations secure, Kevin had become bitter with God. Suppose he refused to feel God's care.

Most likely, he never would have trusted Jesus as Savior. He would be facing a God-less eternity. Think how that would have thwarted God's design for Him and even God's way of using a terrible circumstance to rescue Kevin.

Trust in God even in the middle of the worst times. He cares, and He wants to pour out blessings—sometimes eternal and sometimes temporal—on you.

The Bible Addresses God's Care

"All the ways of the Lord are loving and faithful for those who keep the demands of his covenant." (Psalm 25:10)

"God is faithful in all he does." (Psalm 33:4)

"Because of the Lord's great love we are not consumed, for his compassions never fail. They are new every morning. Great is your faithfulness." (Lamentations 3:22–23)

"'Why do you ask me about what is good?' Jesus replied. 'There is only One who is good.'" (Matthew 19:17)

8

Katie Feenstra

Accepting God's Plan

"For I know the plans I have for you," declares the Lord,
"plans to prosper you and not to harm you."
—*Jeremiah 29:11*

PICTURE THIS:

A family arrives at Applebee's. No big deal. Happens all the time.

Except that this family garners a bit of attention when they show up for honey-grilled salmon. As they walk in the door, first comes Dad. He's seven feet tall. Then comes Mom at six foot four. Then the kids. Matt's six foot nine, who comes with his wife—the only non-six-footer among the adults, followed by Meribeth, who goes about six foot eight, with her husband, Seth. He's six foot ten. Then comes the baby of the family—Katie. She, like her sister, is six foot eight.

Heads turn as the hostess takes the Feenstra family to their seats. Until they are seated, people whisper. People point. People wonder if some male–female basketball team bus just showed up.

Imagine this scenario being repeated day after day after day in your life.

Imagine not being able to go to the mall without everyone looking at you, asking questions. Staring. Imagine trying to go to JCPenney for slacks and discovering that every pair is several inches too short.

Welcome to Katie Feenstra's world.

Katie has been turning heads on the basketball court since she was a rather tall eighth-grader at Grand Rapids Baptist Middle School in Grand Rapids, Michigan. First, people would notice that she was tall. Then, if they stuck around to watch—and they usually did—they would notice that she was a pretty good basketball player.

Smooth. Coordinated. Not awkward. Katie had college scouts crawling all over themselves to get her attention by the time she was a six-foot-eight freshman sharing the court with her senior sister, Meribeth. The tandem led their team to a number one rating in the state, and they went to the quarterfinals as the tallest tandem in Michigan basketball history.

Was it all good for Katie, though? Was it all fun and games to be a foot taller than everyone else? Was it problematic to go to the homecoming banquet at school with someone eight inches shorter?

Was life just a good news–bad news joke for Katie? Good news: You're getting a basketball scholarship. Bad news: Everybody's going to stare and gawk at you.

One advantage of having tall parents, of course, is that this scenario is not new to them. Katie's mom and dad had already been through this a million times by the time she began to notice that her height got people's attention. So when it began to happen, she had someplace to go for help.

"I didn't feel self-conscious about my height until about the seventh grade," Feenstra says. "That's when people started noticing that I was really tall for my age. The attention that I got from my height was more than I could bear at times."

Young teen girls have enough trouble coping with all of the changes that are happening to them without having a built-in attention-getting device thrown into the mix.

"Shopping was a stressful situation," Feenstra recalls. "Trying to find the trendy jeans and shoes that all the other girls had was tough."

Slowly, though, as Katie's mom and dad coached her through those difficult times, Katie gained a new perspective that began to help her cope.

"My parents told Meribeth and me that God made us this height, and He did it for a reason. Back then, that answer was hard to hear, because it did not fix the problem of all the attention. Plus, I still did not know the reason that the Lord had for making me this height."

What began to help Katie figure things out was a verse that many people have discovered to be a source of hope in God's sovereignty. "I always knew that the Lord had my life planned out for me. I clung to Jeremiah 29:11, 'For I know the plans I have for you,' and whenever I felt a little surprised that the Lord would make me this tall, I was always reminded that it was not surprising to the Lord."

God may have known His plans for Katie, and He surely did not create her to be who she was to bring her harm, but this didn't make things any easier for her. And while that verse may have been of comfort to Katie while she and her family were seated around the kitchen table, it was a bit harder to apply once they walked out the door.

"I don't want to sound like being tall was easy. Being tall made life more of a challenge. I was upset when people would laugh or talk behind my back and think I did not hear them."

One of her former teammates in high school recalls some of the ways Katie and her sister Meribeth had to endure life in the heights.

"Whenever we would go anywhere," their former teammate says, "as soon as we would pass, they would make comments. They acted like she didn't have ears. They'd say, 'Man, look at her! Did you see how tall she was?'

"We'd go into McDonald's, and people would bug her and ask her questions. 'How tall are you?' 'Do you play basketball?' 'Can you dunk?' "

Even when Katie was on the court, her definite place of comfort and solace, the comments continued.

"No wonder she can score. She's so tall!"

Or whenever she'd grab a rebound standing behind someone, even if she didn't touch the player, some fan would yell, "Over the back!" as if there were some kind of air rights over the poor girl who was just five foot ten.

Unfortunately, it was lost on many people that Feenstra was not just tall—she was good. She was so good that she set school records for points in a game with 42—twice. And she was so good that when it came time to pick a college to attend, the field was wide open. She could go anywhere she wanted, because everyone seemed to want her.

"When I started playing basketball," she says, "things were supposed to get easier because I was using my height for God's glory. But now I had to pick a college. Plus, I had everyone watching me and observing how I lived my life."

Perhaps by now you know what school Katie chose. And it may be because you were watching in 2005 when she led her team to its first-ever appearance in the NCAA Division I Sweet 16. Just after her team defeated Penn State to join the fifteen other top schools in the country in the tournament, a reporter shoved a microphone in front of an exultant Katie Feenstra and asked, "Katie, you could have gone to any university in the country. Why Liberty?" referring to Liberty University, a strong Christian college in Lynchburg, Virginia.

Katie smiled her beautiful smile and said, "Why not Liberty?! I love it!"

She was doing what her parents had taught her to do early in her life, which is, as she describes it, to "show Christ through basketball."

Despite the troubles of being tall, Katie has discovered that part of the plan God has for her is to use her prodigious basketball skills and her God-given height to glorify God.

And that plan would allow her to move from her Liberty University experience to something that many young girls dream of—a career in the WNBA. Not many kids from small Christian high schools get this kind of opportunity, so Feenstra cherishes what has happened. In the spring of 2005, she was drafted by the Connecticut Sun of the WNBA and traded to the San Antonio Silver Stars. There she has had a chance to extend her testimony for Jesus Christ, even sharing a stage with San Antonio icon David Robinson for a gospel presentation.

Older, more mature, and wiser for her experiences, Feenstra calmly says, "Now whenever I am unsure about my future plans, I don't get too stressed about it because the Lord has everything planned out for me.

"The funny thing is, I am not six-eight to my family and friends. To them, I am just a normal girl. My family and friends always told me that I was beautiful and that God had huge plans for my life, but I had to believe it as true." Now that she does, life is so much better.

And, in case you were wondering (and don't deny it), yes, she has found that special guy. "The Lord has given me self-confidence, and a great guy (who is shorter than I am)."

And then she says this, which says it all: "I love being six-eight. I feel that sometimes being this tall I gain respect from people. I use my height to glorify God through playing a game and showing others how important the Lord is to me. I love it when people ask me if I play basketball now. I can say, 'I sure do!' Then I tell them about my great experiences in the WNBA!

"Who could ask for a better life!"

Looking Up

Let's be honest. We all have things we don't like about ourselves. Or things we don't like about our lives. If we were in charge, we'd sure do things differently.

How about listing a few of them.

Too short. Too fat. Too skinny. Afraid of crowds. Afraid of spiders. Too poor. Too friendly. Full of anxiety. Have dyslexia. Have ADD. Have bad skin. Can't make friends. Can't remember names. Have a crummy job. Suffering from grief. Suffering from depression.

_____. That's a space for the thing you don't like about the way things are.

Katie's problem cannot be avoided, even though she has learned to "avoid places that I think I would get too much attention." But what she has done with help from her parents, her friends, and her God, is to turn what may be seen as a negative into a positive.

There is not a simpler, more profound way to accept God's dealings in our lives. Those who suffer grief sometimes are able to glorify God by helping others who grieve. Those who have disabilities sometimes work hard to overcome them so they can teach younger people to cope. Usually there is a way to use what God has given you and turn it around for His glory.

But to do that we have to take a couple of positive steps. We must trust God when He says He is in control. We have to accept that God does have plans for us; He will guide us. Then we have to trust that His plans are not there to harm us. We have to accept that whatever He does is "for the good of those who love Him" (Romans 8:28).

Think about what you don't like about yourself or your life. Then turn it over to God, thank Him for it, and ask Him to turn it into good.

The Bible Addresses Guidance

"Be strong and take heart, all of you who hope in the Lord." (Psalm 31:24)

"Why are you downcast, O my soul? Why so disturbed within me? Put your hope in God, for I will yet praise him, my Savior and my God." (Psalm 42:5–6)

"Whether you turn to the right or to the left, your ears will hear a voice behind you, saying, 'This is the way; walk in it.'" (Isaiah 30:21)

"The Lord will guide you always; he will satisfy your needs in a sun-scorched land and will strengthen your frame." (Isaiah 58:11)

9

LaDainian Tomlinson

Compassion Starts at Home

Carry each other's burdens, and in this way you will fulfill the law of Christ.
—Galatians 6:2

JUST LOOK AT THAT GUY WITH THE FOOTBALL.
He's cradling the pigskin in his right arm, and he's looking just a few feet
ahead of him. He's looking for daylight—running room—but closing in on
him fast are about nine hundred pounds of linemen.

Just look at his arms. Muscles tense for the impact—and quite impressive muscles they are. Tape encircles his upper arm—tape that was clean and
straight before the game started. Now it's ripped and filthy, battered by close
contact with behemoths from the other side. Other hunks of tape cover his
elbows, trying to protect them for the many times he will be dragged to the
ground this day.

Just look at that uniform. Stained with grass and sweat—and it looks
like a little blood is on there too. Dirtied from an afternoon of brutal combat and teeth-rattling collisions.

This is one tough human. On a Sunday afternoon, he will crash into
and through opposing tacklers, sometimes dragging a couple of them with
him as he chews up yardage. Thirty times or so he will bull his way, feet
churning, through a band of warriors who want nothing better than to strip
the ball from his clutches and bury him under a mountain of tacklers.

During the 2004 NFL season, LaDainian Tomlinson endured the pain
of being a running back on a professional football team to the tune of 1,335
yards and 17 touchdowns. By the sheer force of his steely will and the
improved play of his teammates, the San Diego Chargers made the playoffs.

Good times were coming to San Diego, in part because of Tomlinson's
outstanding talent for slashing through NFL defenses. But even more good
times were in store for Team Tomlinson. For, even as the 2004 season and
dreams of reaching the Super Bowl ended on a negative note—a 20–17
overtime loss to the New York Jets—Tomlinson knew that something really
good was about to happen.

As much as he desired success for the Chargers, as hard as he worked
and as much punishment as he endured to help make it happen, La-

Dainian's really big deal that year was going on at home. As one of his teammates told the battered and defeated running back in the locker room after the loss to New York, "Remember, you're going to be a daddy."

LaDainian's wife, LaTorsha, was pregnant with a girl. They had already named her, even though her birth was not on the docket until several months later.

McKiah Renee Tomlinson. That was what Team Tomlinson would call their little girl. And this strong, relentless runner with the all-world stats and the all-man tats couldn't wait to hold her, kiss her, talk to her, and spoil her like any first-time daddy does.

"I'm going to give that child a lot of love. Just a lot of love."

That was in December 2004.

In February, LaDainian headed west to Hawaii to play in his second straight Pro Bowl.

How could life improve for the former Texas Christian University star? He was in Hawaii with his pregnant wife and with his offensive line, for whom he paid the way to join him in paradise.

But then something terrible happened. A couple of weeks after LaTorsha and LaDainian returned to their home in Poway, outside San Diego, their world was flipped upside down. On February 22, 2005, the young couple discovered that McKiah would never share the huge new house LaDainian had built for their family. The baby that would make them Mommy and Daddy was dead. LaTorsha delivered the baby, but not to the excited welcome they had anticipated.

And now it was up to LaDainian to figure out a way to redirect his love for McKiah into compassion and care for his wife. While he was devastated by the loss of his baby, he knew that LaTorsha would need extra measures of his concern—his love—his tender voice of comfort.

But how could he? How could he face this trial in a way that would protect and nurture his grieving wife?

He would do so by leaning on a faith that he had developed before the tragedy struck. A friend of Tomlinson's observed that the way he was able to be the strength for his wife after her miscarriage was "developed by a life of faith; it doesn't just happen when trials happen."

As a high schooler, Tomlinson had grown cocky because of his prodigious talent, but he didn't like the person he was becoming. After all, his mom had taken him to church his whole life, and he knew the truth about Jesus Christ. But he hadn't personalized it.

"I felt like I needed my own personal relationship with God, so I didn't have to rely on what my mom said all the time." So he trusted Christ.

That relationship would be the bedrock when his life was rocked with the loss of his unborn daughter.

"Sometimes you forget that you're not in control," he said of those difficult days. He had been so certain that "I'm going to be a father and do this for my child, do this for my wife . . ."

What LaDainian ended up doing for his wife was help her through that most difficult time.

"I think the biggest thing for my wife was just trying to be strong for her," LaDainian told a reporter a couple of months after the miscarriage. "You don't want to see your wife breaking down. You have to be strong for her."

That was just what she needed.

"I was a wreck," she would say many months later. "LaDainian is my rock. He sacrificed his own need to grieve, pushed it to the back, to stand up and be there for me."

Not every husband would do that. Not every man understands the significance of being tough at the job while still being soft-hearted and compassionate at home. Not every husband turns hard times into a chance for his wife to reflect back with words such as, "God definitely used LaDainian for me."

But LaDainian had helped, and LaTorsha knew where that help came from. "I know that God was telling him, 'She's going to need you.' I'll be honest: I was angry. It took LaDainian to tell me, 'God has a plan.'"

The bruising running back reminded LaTorsha of that a few months after McKiah's passing. LaTorsha was lying in bed and, as is so normal for those in grief, she was unable to get up. The pain was simply too great for her to bear at that moment.

The man they call LT sat down beside her and spoke quietly with her—listening some and talking some. But the thing she remembered most about that conversation was her husband's reminder that even though the two of them did not understand the overall purpose and picture God was putting together for their life, He knew. God knew.

"He knows everything," Tomlinson says.

God even knows how to guide a muscle-bound NFL superstar to come gently beside his grieving wife and pour out enough compassion and love to lift her from her despair.

That LT took up the challenge to help LaTorsha is how we know he's a man—not because he can lead the NFL in rushing.

Looking Up

Is LaDainian Tomlinson a rarity? Is it unusual for macho guys, strong guys, tough guys to be tender guys as well?

In reality, it doesn't matter, does it? It doesn't matter what the norm is—what the average on this is. It only matters that you, if you are a male, do as the Bible instructs regarding caring for others.

Look, for instance, at the passage of Scripture that describes what took place when Jesus faced grief head on. His friends Martha, Mary, and Lazarus lived in Bethany, not far from Jerusalem. Jesus was away on a ministry trip when word came that Lazarus was ill. By the time Jesus returned, Lazarus had died.

Jesus saw the sadness in Mary and Martha, and He sensed His own sorrow at this event. So how did He respond? He cried.

"Jesus wept," John 11:35 tells us. Jesus, the great creator—the One who would soon be bringing Lazarus back to life—cried. No pride here in standing strong in the face of sadness. No, Jesus cried.

Jesus was one strong Man. Had to be just to carry that cross up the hill. Had to be just to put up with insults while on trial for doing nothing wrong. Had to be to hang there in the worst kind of agony and say, "Forgive them. They don't know what they are doing."

Strong Jesus cried. Strong Jesus wept. And strong Jesus loved.

When Paul wanted to put into words how much a man should love his wife, he used Jesus as the example. "Husbands," the great missionary said, "love your wives just as Christ loved the church and gave himself up for her" (Ephesians 5:25).

That's an example guys can use even if marriage is farther from their mind than Mars.

The strong love that LaDanian showed for his wife, and the deep, emotional love Jesus showed for the people around Him, isn't just something reserved for Mom and Dad.

Sacrificial love can include the way you give yourself up for friends. It can be seen in the way you give up summer vacation to take a mission trip. It can be seen in backing down on some bug-your-parents issue just to show them that you love and appreciate all they've done for you. And strong love is the kind that never ever allows you to hurt a young woman by taking advantage of her in any way possible when you are on a date.

Are you macho, man? Show it by being strong enough to practice godly love toward everyone around you. That's the best way to show that you want to honor your Savior by being like Him.

The Bible Addresses Sorrow and Compassion

"Blessed are those who mourn, for they will be comforted." (Matthew 5:4)

"Mourn with those who mourn." (Romans 12:15)

"Husbands, love your wives and do not be harsh with them." (Colossians 3:19)

"Finally, all of you, live in harmony with one another . . . be compassionate and humble." (1 Peter 3:8)

10

Paul Byrd

Paying Tribute

The elders who direct the affairs of the church well
are worthy of double honor.
—*1 Timothy 1:17*

BASEBALL PLAYERS HAVE BEEN KNOWN TO
make up some unusual on-field displays in order to try to convey a message.

Some will point to the sky when they hit a home run, leaving the fans
to wonder exactly what is meant by that sky-point. Is it a way of honoring
someone who has gone on before—a father, perhaps?

Some will pause briefly before stepping into the batter's box to make a
religious gesture of some kind. For many, it is a kind of quick prayer—an
acknowledgment at least of God's presence in their lives.

Others have pointed to their heart as if to say to fans, "I appreciate
you." Still others have developed quick hand signs to tell friends or family
members watching at home that they are thinking of them, like Michelle
Kwan's ear-pull signal in the kiss and cry area.

Major league pitcher Paul Byrd is usually not a signaler. The veteran
right-hander, who has been a workhorse pitcher for several baseball teams
since being drafted out of Louisiana State University, is a no-nonsense
worker out there on the mound. He's not usually given to any kind of public display other than just hard work and hard throwing.

That changed briefly in 2005.

That was the summer Byrd made his living as a pitcher for the Los
Angeles Angels of Anaheim. The Angels were Byrd's fifth major league team.
After making it to the big time in 1995, Byrd had played for the New York
Mets, Atlanta Braves, Philadelphia Phillies, Kansas City Royals, and the
Angels.

At each of those stops along the major league way, Byrd had the opportunity to get involved in the efforts of Baseball Chapel. Each major league
team allows a Baseball Chapel representative to head up a program of Bible
study or Sunday services or both. Byrd, a Christian, took advantage of that
opportunity. In doing so, he got to know very well a number of chaplains—
men who would hold services and lead studies to help the Christian players

keep strong spiritually throughout the season.

Good men all, these spiritual mentors gave their time to make sure believers did not neglect their growth as followers of Jesus Christ.

But when Byrd arrived in Anaheim to play for the Angels, he got to meet a very special Baseball Chapel representative—a guy by the name of Chuck Obremski.

Obremski was a pastor first—heading up the growing community of believers at Kindred Community Church in the city that boasts the West Coast version of the Magic Kingdom. From the pulpit of that church, Obremski preached the message that he had wholeheartedly accepted in 1978—that he was a sinner who could be saved by God's grace. His enthusiasm for life and for Jesus Christ endeared him to his church members and to a cadre of professional athletes.

Chuck worked with the L.A. Rams before they headed east. He guided the Mighty Ducks of the NHL. But perhaps his most valued moment was when the Angels gave him a World Series ring to thank him for being such an integral part of their 2002 World Series championship.

Indeed, Obremski was loved by many—by any who came into contact with him and his contagious faith.

But when Paul Byrd finally came on board for the Angels and got to be under Obremski's tutelage spiritually, the gentle preacher was not the man he once had been. An aggressive cancer had erupted in his body, and throughout the 2005 season, his condition continued to deteriorate.

Despite the debilitation that resulted from Chuck's cancer, he continued to serve the Angels. He continued to conduct chapel services and provide spiritual help for Byrd and his teammates—right up until his wasted body wouldn't allow it anymore.

So it was, that on September 19, 2005, at 1:05 P.M. Pacific time, when Paul Byrd strolled toward the mound to start a game against the Detroit Tigers, the pitcher's heart was heavy with sorrow. It was clear to everyone who knew Obremski that his time on earth could now be recorded in hours—perhaps even minutes.

Byrd knew that his mentor was near the end, but he thought that perhaps Pastor Chuck would rally enough to watch the game on television. It was Sunday, and Obremski would usually have conducted a chapel service for the team. But on this Sunday, Byrd knew, Chaplain Chuck's next singing would probably be done in heaven.

So Byrd, hoping that Obremski was watching, put together a gesture perhaps never displayed by a baseball player. He raised his hands above his head and touched the tip of his glove with the tip of his right fingers—making a perfect O with his arms as a way of saying, "I'm thinking about you, Chuck."

Byrd went on to pitch into the seventh inning of that game that day, and when he left the contest, he reprised his tribute to Obremski, again making an overhead O as he strolled toward the dugout.

Paul Byrd wanted his chaplain to see these tributes—the one at the beginning of the game and the one when he was taken out for a relief pitcher. What he could not know was this: If Chuck Obremski did see Byrd's thoughtful gestures, he did not see them on TV. You see, the moment Paul Byrd thought to pay tribute to his friend in the first inning was the moment Chuck Obremski was busy entering eternity. He died at 1:05.

At that moment, Pastor O probably didn't care much about baseball anymore, for he was about to meet Jesus.

While one man was paying tribute from his heart to the tips of his fingers, the man he was honoring was stepping on shore in his heavenly home—where he would receive the truest and best tribute from the lips of his Savior: "Well done, good and faithful servant."

Looking Up

Church leadership is not easy. It comes connected with all kinds of obstacles. Any time a person feels called to lead a body of Christians, he knows he will face differences of opinion, interpersonal relationships, and sometimes even jealousy of his leadership.

That's why, as the beneficiaries of their work, we need to pay tribute to our leaders. One way to do that is to make sure their material needs are met. That's the message of 1 Timothy 5:17, when it was suggested that the church leaders get "double honor."

But there is so much more. Each year in October, many churches celebrate Clergy Appreciation Week. It's a special time when churches can do something special to tell their shepherd that the flock is behind him.

One church arranged for the members to buy books and other study materials the pastor would want. Another sent the family on a much-needed vacation. Perhaps your church is a part of this kind of tribute.

Mixed in with an assortment of admonitions at the end of 1 Thessalonians, Paul says this: "Now we ask you, brothers, to respect those who work hard among you, who are over you in the Lord and who admonish you. Hold them in highest regard in love because of their work" (5:12–13).

It's clear that the apostle is challenging Christians to show love and care for the leaders in the church. And it's clear that we should, as Paul Byrd did, find ways to honor our spiritual mentors.

Let's search out methods of doing that this week. Waiting too long might rob both us and our leaders of the shared joy of paying tribute and giving honor to those to whom honor is due.

The Bible Addresses Giving Honor

"Welcome [Epaphroditus] in the Lord with great joy, and honor men like him, because he almost died for the work of Christ." (Philippians 2:29–30)

"Now we ask you, brothers, to respect those who work hard among you, who are over you in the Lord and who admonish you." (1 Thessalonians 5:12)

"The elders who direct the affairs of the church well are worthy of double honor, especially those whose work is preaching and teaching." (1 Timothy 5:17)

11

Hunter and Val Kemper
God's Mysterious Goodness

Many are the plans in a man's heart,
but it is the Lord's purpose that prevails.
—Proverbs 19:21

IMAGINE FOR A MOMENT BEING NUMBER ONE
in the world at something.

The best there is. The top dog. The cream of the crop.

For most of us, who were never even the best in our grade at anything, that's a steep climb up the ladder of imagination.

That exalted perch, though, is exactly where a man named Hunter Kemper found himself in the year 2005.

Number one in the world.

Perhaps you are racking your brain to recall why it is Hunter stood astride the world.

Basketball? No, that's LeBron. Or Tim. Or Dwyane.

Football? Nope. Peyton. Shaun. Reggie.

Baseball? Uh-uh. Albert. Alex.

Try triathlon. Swimming. Biking. Running. All in the same event.

That is Hunter Kemper's sport. And in 2005, he was ranked the number one triathlete on this big blue marble.

For a long time, Hunter Kemper was alone in his pursuit of Olympic and other competitive success. He was driven to become a great triathlete— to turn his successful running career at Wake Forest University into a top-of-the-ladder triathlon career. And when you're on your way to the top, sometimes stopping along the way to start a relationship might just slow you down.

Let's leave Hunter on his climb and turn our attention to another world-class athlete. Valerie Sterk had made a name for herself in volleyball with an All-American career at Michigan State University.

She began playing volleyball when she was eight years old, became a star at South Christian High School in Grand Rapids, Michigan, and then twice was named All-American while at Michigan State. While she was spiking for the Spartans, they made one trip to the NCAA Final Four.

Val's successful college career propelled her to a spot on the U.S. National team. For three years, she dedicated herself to helping the United States win Olympic gold. Along the way, she saw the world as the team traveled to Australia, China, Europe, and the Dominican Republic. For those three years, she did whatever was asked of her—often practicing thirty-six hours a week.

Less than a year before the 2000 Olympics, a stunning visit to the doctor's office nearly derailed her volleyball dreams. When her physician took a seemingly harmless mole off Val's arm, he discovered that there was nothing benign about it. He diagnosed her with malignant melanoma—a skin cancer that is often fatal. Three weeks later, a more complete surgical procedure took place, and she was declared free of cancer.

Her life was secure. But her spot on the volleyball team wasn't.

In the summer of 2000, just weeks before the women's team was set to head for the Olympics, the coach had a decision to make. He had fifteen superstar volleyball players on his team, and he could pick only twelve of them to wear the hallowed red, white, and blue uniforms of the USA.

Val recalls what happened. "He listed the names and left the room. I thought there was a mistake. There were twelve names, and 'Val Sterk' was not listed. How could this be? Some of the players on the list had been with the team for only a couple of months; I had been there for years! My heart was broken; my dreams, crushed. My dream to play volleyball in the Olympics was shattered."

Val, it appeared, would not be going to Australia.

The volleyball team had been training in Colorado Springs, Colorado. Of course, they weren't the only athletes there. Every day the Olympic Training Center cafeteria was filled with athletes from a number of sports, all doing the same thing: getting something to eat. Okay, all doing the same thing: working and sweating and striving for Olympic glory.

One of those teams was the triathlon development team.

One day, a tall, athletic young man from Florida noticed a tall, athletic young woman from Michigan.

At the time, Hunter Kemper was not the number one triathlete in the world. He was working hard to get to the Olympics—just as Val had been doing. He, however, would be successful in getting there.

Val and Hunter had seen each other occasionally at the home of a Colorado Springs couple who ministered to Olympic athletes through Young Life. On Fridays Mark and Peggy Henjum would have a get-together for the athletes. At one of those Friday socials, Hunter had planned to ask Valerie on a date—but he chickened out.

The next day, Hunter was on a biking workout when he stopped at the Henjums' house to talk with them. Val was on the phone with Peggy—working up the courage to tell her the bad news about being cut from the team. But matchmaker Peggy didn't wait to hear what Val had to say. She put Hunter on the phone and coached him as he asked Val out on a date.

She said yes, so on the very same day that a long-term relationship with the U.S. volleyball team ended, God put a brand-new relationship in Val's life. And, of course, this one won't be destroyed by a coach's decision.

Later, Val would write about this unusual stream of events this way: "That disappointing day in 2000 had a bright ending. Three years later, I would marry the man of my dreams, Hunter Kemper. Now I know why God had me at the Olympic Training Center all those years."

After that first date on the worst/best day of Val's life, the relationship took off in a hurry. Notably, Hunter invited Val to travel with his family to Sydney to watch him compete in the Olympic Games. So although this wasn't the way she envisioned it, Valerie did get to the Olympics.

Three years later, the two were married in Val's home church in Byron Center, Michigan. That day, a family came into being, and a family legend was born—the Legend of the Krispy Kreme doughnuts. Hunter had already displayed a propensity for the sweet treats, and he thought it would be a special treat if everyone at the reception could enjoy them as well. So besides carrot cake, those assembled at the wedding got Krispy Kreme doughnuts—the original glazed, of course, which are Hunter's favorites.

A little less than two years later, Kemper became the number one triathlete in the world. He didn't credit a doughy confection for his climb to the top, but he credited Val for having a huge role in his winning. "She's a big reason I'm racing so well," he has said. "She knows what it takes to be an Olympic athlete. She has helped me keep going in the right direction."

In the summer of 2000, Kemper was trying to make a breakthrough in his sport and Val was trying to recover from the shock of being bounced from hers. But somehow God's timing put them together at just the right time—the right time to help both of them succeed in life and in faith.

"From the beginning, Val and I have talked about wanting people to see Christ in our relationship."

Being number one is nice, but knowing that God has put life together for you in His timing is even better.

Looking Up

Philip Yancey has correctly noted that we see God's will best in the rearview mirror. Often it is only as we look back that we see how well God has orchestrated our lives to serve Him and honor Him.

The intriguing story of Joseph in the Old Testament illustrates that we must trust God that He has a plan—that He knows what He is doing—when we think everything is all out of whack. After all, how can it be good to have all of your brothers turn on you so drastically that they sell you to some strangers who happen by on camels?

Joseph surely had to be thinking: God, did you forget about me?

Yet that road to Egypt would eventually bring his entire family back to him in a way that still touches our hearts today.

God's timing was perfect. He needed to have Joseph exactly where he was when the famine hit. He gave him wisdom and expertise to save thousands of people.

Val Sterk, like all of us who lose something of great value, had no idea that God could have been orchestrating her day. She didn't know that the same day a coach left her name off a list in what surely looked like a mistake, she would be ready to welcome into her life a young man who could understand her pain and have the spiritual wisdom to help her through it.

When Joseph's brothers finally saw the entire picture that lay before them, they saw that even their own cruelty was used by God to transform Joseph into a leader who could rescue them. Joseph looked over his family and told them that even though they meant their actions for evil, God was able to turn them into good. Only an omniscient, omnipresent God can orchestrate such things. Only His magnificent timing could be so great that even sending along a caravan of greedy traders could be part of a long procession that would lead Joseph's brothers to Egypt and rescue.

Look around at the events in your life. Look in the rearview mirror and notice how God put things together for you. See how His wisdom, which far outdistances ours, puts the puzzle together just as He wants it.

Then trust Him. Trust His heart. Even when you don't understand the moves He makes, trust the wisdom behind those moves.

The Bible Addresses God's Goodness

"Yet he has not left himself without testimony: He has shown kindness by giving you rain from heaven and crops in their seasons; he provides you with plenty of food and fills your hearts with joy." (Acts 14:17)

"Show me your ways, O Lord, teach me your paths; guide me in your truth and teach me, for you are God my Savior, and my hope is in you all day long." (Psalm 25:4-5)

"'I know the plans I have made for you,' declares the Lord, 'plans to prosper you and not to harm you, plans to give you a hope and a future.'" (Jeremiah 29:11)

"Great are the works of the Lord; they are pondered by all who delight in them." (Psalm 111:2)

Tim Tebow

A Sense of Mission

Go into all the world and preach the good news to all creation.
—Mark 16:15

SOME PEOPLE SAY, "YOUTH IS WASTED ON THE young." You and I—and Tim Tebow—know how wrong that can be.

This is one young person who can show the way for the rest of us when it comes to fulfilling one of Jesus' most important commandments.

Yes, Tim Tebow, who in 2006 was just getting started as a college quarterback. Tim Tebow, who was one of the top-five most highly recruited quarterbacks among high schoolers in the United States that year. Tim Tebow, who made a lot of Gators fans happy when he decided go to college in Gainesville, Florida, and toss footballs around for the University of Florida.

See, long before football fans had heard about Tim Tebow and were itching to see him fling the pigskin in college, he had already established himself on a different kind of field.

The mission field.

This is when it stops sounding like a story that will be told in *Sports Illustrated* and starts sounding like a story that should be told in the archives at the Billy Graham Center at Wheaton College.

This left-handed kid, who went to high school at his kitchen table but played football for Nease High School, was born in the faraway country of the Philippines. He was born there because that's where his parents were missionaries. That's where God called Robert Tebow to share the gospel with people who would never hear about Jesus if he didn't tell them.

And that's where Tim Tebow would first make it clear what kind of person he really was.

But first let's go back and see what kind of football player Tebow turned out to be—and why when he decided to play for the University of Florida, so many people saw him as the future.

Just revisit for a minute the Class 4A state championship game for Tebow and his Nease teammates. Playing against the two-time defending champions, Tebow led his team to the title by passing for 237 yards, throwing for four touchdowns, running for 183 yards, and rushing for two touchdowns. Oh, yes, and he also came back on the field and played some defense when that was needed.

That game was the ending of a memorable senior year in which Tebow tallied 3,442 yards in the air, passed for 34 touchdowns, and rushed for 1,045 yards. When you add up his stats throughout his high school years, you get some brand-new records for the state of Florida: 9,840 yards passing; 13,050 total yards of offense; and 159 touchdowns.

So when it comes to football, Tebow certainly established his credentials early. He earned his way to Gainesville.

In addition to being a record-setter on the gridiron, Tebow was also a trendsetter of sorts off the field. He was homeschooled by his parents, but they made sure he found a place where he could develop and display his football skills. So although he didn't attend classes with his Nease High School teammates, he guided them to a state championship. That's not a combination you see often.

And then there is that matter of fulfilling God's commandment. You know, the one about going into all the world to preach the gospel. The Great Commission, it's called.

And just like you've probably never seen a kid play football as Tim does, you probably never saw a kid fulfill God's commission as he has done.

Accompanying his dad on mission trips to the Philippines, Tim did more than stand in the back and look proudly on as his father preached. He would actually go in there and call some audibles.

"In the Philippines," he says about his efforts as a teenager, "I preached to ten thousand high schoolers at one time. It was the biggest high school in that region, and about eight thousand people came forward to accept Christ."

Eight thousand. See? That's Billy Graham-esque.

Eight thousand new recruits for the kingdom. Nine thousand eight-hundred and forty yards for his football team. There's no doubt which stat stands out in Tebow's mind.

"Most of them had never heard the gospel of Christ before, and it was just amazing.

"Ministry has always been tugging at my heart, and what's interesting is that it's just as rewarding to talk to ten thousand people as it is to lead a friend to Christ in a one-on-one situation."

In early 2006, leadership and his ability to speak in public manifested itself in Tebow's life when he had the privilege of addressing his home church upon the retirement of his longtime pastor, Dr. Jerry Vines. Here was a high school kid standing up in front of a congregation of thousands. In the Philippines, they might not have known or cared who Tim was. At First Baptist Church in Jacksonville, he stood before people who had seen him grow up.

He calmly stood before the church and told them, "Pastor Vines always shared the Word of God and shared it like it was coming straight at me. There are a lot of role models, but not a lot of role models of character. Dr. Vines is a man of God."

Tim Tebow is an especially talented young athlete. He also excelled at baseball in high school, where he was an outfielder and a pitcher. Yet he has shown that his true mission falls outside of the sports arena. Although it's pretty clear that barring some major injury he will end up playing NFL football, he has a pretty good backup plan. "For years I've thought about being a missionary."

"I just want to try to be a good example to my teammates and others whether I'm on or off the field. If I can do that and lead others to Christ, then I'll be successful."

When was the last time you heard a highly recruited football star say that?

Looking Up

Let's face it. There aren't many who are anything like Tim Tebow. His high school football stats set him apart from most of us, no matter what sports exploits and highlights we've had. Tebow, in a word, is exceptional.

But if you like football, and if you like to play a little now and then, it's a pretty good guess that when your friends say, "Hey, let's play some football in the backyard," you don't say, "Nah, I can't. I'm not as good as Tim Tebow."

That would be ridiculous.

Similarly, it would be pretty ridiculous to decide that you really can't present the gospel to anyone because you don't have the preaching skills of Tebow. Sure, he can address ten thousand students in the Philippines, and he is to be commended for his poise. But that doesn't make him different from any of us when it comes to fulfilling the Great Commission.

God has called each of us, in one way or another, to make the gospel known to others.

So if someone were to say, "You know, I really don't know much about this Christian stuff. What's the deal?" we can't say, "Uh, I really can't talk about it. I'm not as good as Tim Tebow."

The gospel is the best news that ink has ever printed. It is the plan of God, meant to give life and hope and eternity to everyone who believes. And in God's plan, there is a simple marketing plan to let others know— one believer telling someone who needs to believe.

Sometimes a person comes along who can tell thousands at once, and we can be grateful that happens. But that should never cause us to diminish our own responsibility to preach the gospel wherever we are—even if we can only do it one person at a time.

The Bible Addresses Evangelism

"All authority in heaven and on earth has been given to me. Therefore go and make disciples of all nations, baptizing them in the name of the Father and of the Son and of the Holy Spirit." (Matthew 28:18–19)

"And of this gospel I was appointed a herald and an apostle and a teacher." (2 Timothy 1:11)

"Yet when I preach gospel, I cannot boast, for I am compelled to preach." (1 Corinthians 9:16)

"For we do not preach ourselves, but Jesus Christ as Lord." (2 Corinthians 4:5)

13

Mark Richt

We Are Family

Unless the Lord builds the house, its builders labor in vain.
—*Psalm 127:1*

LET'S JUST FACE IT RIGHT UP FRONT. BEING A major college football coach is probably not too good for family life.

Oh, there are advantages—such as never having to worry about money. And it's probably pretty cool to go to school on Monday after Dad's team has defeated Florida on Saturday.

But realistically, there are probably more drawbacks to being a coach than there are players on the team.

A coach is gone a lot, recruiting or coaching or studying films or speaking at a banquet or meeting with alumni or just trying to figure out how to win.

A coach gets criticized in the papers, on the sports news, and even by just plain old citizens who hardly know a pigskin from a pork rind.

A big-time college coach can't just saunter nonchalantly into the local Chick-fil-A without having everybody and his cousin wanting to talk to him or at least stare at him and whisper, "Doesn't that look like. . . ?"

Yet with all that going on, there's at least one head coach who probably fares better than most in the "living a normal life" category. In this coach's home, there is some pretty cool stuff going on because the coach in question has his priorities right.

And when a father has his priorities right—whether he's the head coach of a Big Ten football team or a third-grade teacher at the local elementary school—things will go pretty well in the family.

Mark Richt is the guy. He's one of those priorities-right kind of dads. And even though he belongs to an entire state, in effect, as a major college football coach, his family knows he's there for them first. Georgia football has his attention, that's for sure. But his family has his heart.

Let's look at how he proves that.

First is something he and his wife Katharyn did in the late 1990s. At the time, Richt was working his way toward a major college coaching position. He had already served as an assistant coach for Bobby Bowden at Florida

State for more than a dozen years. His name was being tossed about as a possible head coach somewhere else. His résumé was building, and he could have been so football-focused that he would be no family-good.

But he wasn't. In fact, when he was not drawing up plays and guiding large college students around a grass-covered field, he and his wife and their two children, John and David, were praying about a possible new development in the family.

"We were in Sunday school class one day talking about the ills of society," Richt is quoted as saying in the Georgia Bulldogs' media guide as he tells about this time in his family's life. "We explored questions like, 'Who's in charge of taking care of the poor and the elderly?' We felt like the church should do its share."

The Richts had heard about a couple of kids who lived in an orphanage in Ukraine, and they began to pray for them. Then the family decided that prayer was not enough. They wanted to go get Zack and Anya and bring them into their home.

So in 1999, Mark and Katharyn left for Ukraine to pick up Zack and Anya. It was not easy. Katharyn had to stay in the country for thirty-one days, and Mark was there for eight days. Finally, in July that year, Jon and David had a new brother and a new sister.

When Katharyn brought them home, the Richts had their work cut out for them. Mark and Katharyn spent a lot of time helping them to understand some things that they hadn't learned in the orphanage—things like right and wrong.

"It took the children time to learn the ropes, to learn the language," Richt told *Sports Spectrum* magazine. "There were a lot of barriers that had to be established and lots of trust and love that had to be developed.

"It wasn't instantaneous," Richt says about that transition. "They knew we were Mom and Dad, but it was very new to them to really trust us." The football thing played into the equation as well, for Mark realized that Katharyn had the advantage of time. "I think it took longer for them to trust me than Katharyn because Katharyn was always with them. She was always the caretaker. I wasn't there as much."

That's another thing that shows how much Mark Richt has nailed his priorities to the right wall. He has a clear admiration for the role his wife plays in their home. He appreciates her.

"She's a strong, independent woman, but she's a Spirit-filled woman," Richt says proudly. "She allows God to work in her life and control her attitudes if she has an attitude about something. She's very submissive to God to allow Him to shape her in the way she should be."

Richt loves kids. He loves his wife.

But, hey, he's a football coach. Isn't this the part where the dad-coach shuts the door of the house and forgets about the family? You know, sleep at the office in a cot and not see the kids between July and December?

Not Richt. One of the things he does to make sure family is first is to have his morning staff meetings late enough so that dads can help get the kids out of the house and off to school in the morning. He also plans a family night when the coaches bring their families in to have dinner with the players—building, not tearing down relationships.

Lunch with Katharyn—even during the heavy practice times.

Visiting the kids at school for lunch.

Dinner with the family or just with Katharyn in the evening.

And then what about free time? Even then, Richt tries to use that for his family instead of always being out on the golf course or spending it on other personal down times. And when he does hit the links, sometimes he takes the kids with him.

Mark Richt is a leader of men. He knows that to teach young men to become the best they can be on the field and later in life, he must lead with loyalty, integrity, hard work, and honesty. But he also is teaching them, perhaps without a word, that a real man takes care of his family first.

And as he does that, he is proving that being an excellent college football coach can also mean being a dad with the right priorities at home.

Looking Up

One famous NFL coach famously said that he was not going to let his relationship with his wife get in the way of being a successful coach. So one year when the chips were down, his wife left him. And he was okay with that. The most precious relationship he could have with another human was trashed for the sake of a game. That coach is no longer coaching.

Let's count the many ways we can push aside those closest to us so we can do something of far less importance than they are. Being too driven to be the big star in everything at school might leave you with fewer friends. Pushing yourself to grow up too fast may make you think you don't need your parents' advice. Becoming obsessed with material things might distract you from your relationship with God.

Notice how that kind of situation contrasts with the hopeful words of Psalm 128. There we read about a person who walks in the ways of God, who eats the fruit of His labor. This man, who lives by God's standards, enjoys the relationship with his wife and is proud of his children. Because he fears the Lord—and consequently cares properly for his family—he is blessed.

While you are young, establish this principle in your heart. Following godly standards and seeking family love are vital to true happiness.

That kind of action leads to God's smile of approval.

What have you done today to put your priorities in the order you think God would have you put them?

The Bible Addresses Family

"Sons are a heritage from the Lord, children a reward from him." (Psalm 127:3)

"A greedy man brings trouble to his family." (Proverbs 15:27)

"A wife of noble character . . . [and] her husband. . . ." (Read about them in Proverbs 31:10–31)

"If anyone sets his heart on being an overseer . . . he must manage his own family well and see that his children obey him with proper respect." (1 Timothy 3:1, 4)

14

Shanna Zolman and Sidney Spencer
More Than Teammates

Perfume and incense bring joy to the heart, and the pleasantness
of one's friend springs from his earnest counsel.
—*Proverbs 27:9*

TO ANYONE WHO EVER PLAYED TEAM SPORTS
and was issued a uniform, it is abundantly clear that the number on that
uniform becomes forever a part of who you are. When players are honored
by their teams, what do they do? They retire their uniform number.

Number 3

Number 7

Number 23

Number 33

We know them by their number.

Babe Ruth

Mickey Mantle

Michael Jordan

Kareem Abdul-Jabaar

So what Shanna Zolman did for Sidney Spencer in the late winter of
2005 shows something special about their friendship.

Zolman and Spencer became friends as teammates on the University of
Tennessee women's basketball team.

Not at first, mind you. At first, when Sidney Spencer rolled into Knoxville, Shanna didn't quite know what to make of the new girl from down
south. Sidney has been known to operate as if from a different planet.

"I'm on my own cloud," she's been known to say.

The girl named Sid is a free spirit who was not afraid to express herself
from the moment she walked on campus.

"We didn't know if she was going to stay," recalls Zolman. "She was off
to herself. I didn't know her at all."

Zolman, a sharpshooting guard from Wawasee High School in Syracuse,
Indiana, had gone to the University of Tennessee to try to win a national
championship.

What she got was a best friend.

It wasn't long before Zolman found out that Spencer, a forward from Alabama, shared something better than basketball. They shared a love for Jesus Christ.

And a love for missions.

In the summer of 2004, the two of them got out of town. They went to the Dominican Republic with Score International, a Chattanooga-based missions organization that helps young people get their feet wet in missions.

It was on that venture that Shanna saw the advantage of Sidney's personality. Her free-wheeling way of dealing with people made it easy for her to share the gospel. "I admire her for her boldness," Zolman would say of Spencer's ability to communicate—even when she and her listeners don't speak the same language.

When Shanna and Sidney returned from that trip in 2004, they set out to help the Tennessee Lady Vols on their quest for a national championship.

But that year did not turn out as they hoped. A key reason was injuries. For one thing, new recruit and highly regarded center Candace Parker suffered an injury that caused her to miss her freshman year. Then later in the season, the injury bug bit Sidney.

It was late February, and the Lady Vols were at practice. Sidney went down in pain, and when team physician Dr. Rebecca Morgan looked her over, she suspected a ligament tear. An MRI revealed she was right. Spencer would miss the remainder of the season with an ACL tear in her right knee.

Coach Pat Summitt said of Spencer's injury, "I hate this for Sid and our program. She's played some of her best basketball in the past couple of weeks."

The news hit Sid's buddy Shanna especially hard. So hard that she felt she had to do something to honor Sidney.

So what did Shanna Zolman do? She set aside her own uniform number—the number 5 that she had so proudly worn and had so capably represented for nearly three seasons. She did that so she could wear number 1, her friend Sidney's number. She sacrificed her own fame, in a way, and the recognition she had built up over the years and wore number 1 to shine the light on her fallen friend.

For Summitt, who had seen just about everything in her decades of coaching more than a thousand college basketball games, this was a new one. When Shanna approached Coach Summitt to ask her if she could switch numbers to pay homage to her friend, Summitt asked, "Is it legal?"

"I had never had a player want to change numbers in the middle of a year," she told the *Knoxville News Sentinel.* Indeed, it was an unprecedented request.

"It touched me," Summitt concluded. "They are great friends."

It also touched Lady Vols fans. One who posted a comment on a Web site dedicated to the team said, "I hate it so bad for Sidney, but isn't it so incredible to have such a great friend as Shanna."

Sidney thought so too. When her friend took off her warm-ups and she saw that Shanna was wearing her uniform number, Zolman says, "She started bawling."

Friendships are such awesome relationships, and one reason is because they evoke such sympathy and such warm feelings of concern. Sidney and Shanna were two young women, bound together by faith and shared mission and deep concern for each other. That's why when Sidney got hurt, Shanna says, "It hurt so bad. Part of me went down."

And both were lifted up by Shanna's surprising gesture of keeping Sidney's number in the forefront as she rehabbed her surgically repaired knee.

In 2005, the young women took off again for the mission field. This time they headed to Costa Rica. For Sidney, it was a purpose-driven trip. "I learned why I play basketball," she says. "It's not for me. It's for God and His purpose and will in my life."

While there, they shared their basketball skills, spoke often about Jesus, visited orphanages, and took food to the homeless.

But as friends will do—especially young friends with a sense of adventure—they ventured out of the safe zone. Surely they didn't tell Coach Summitt that one of their favorite adventures was grabbing a zip line that coursed through the rain forest—riding it at fifty-five miles an hour from the top of a mountain, through the trees, and to the forest floor below. Now, that's a mission trip!

Shanna Zolman and Sidney Spencer. It's easy to see that no matter what their uniforms say, they are both young women who rate number one.

Looking Up

Shanna and Sidney. Jonathan and David. See the similarities? Two people who became great friends and who went out of their way to help each other.

What's not to like about the Old Testament story of Jonathan and David?

What's not to like about David going to Jonathan and honestly explaining his fear that Jonathan's father wanted to kill David—and then having Jonathan say, "Whatever you want me to do, I'll do for you"?

Have you ever gotten a call from someone who said, "Hey, can you do me a favor?"

That kind of open-ended question can be answered yes if the person asking it is a trusted friend. If not—if the person asking is just an acquaintance in which you have little time or friendship invested—you might be left wondering, *Will this person ask me something that is more than I am willing to do for an acquaintance?*

But if someone you know as you would know a brother or sister asks you that, you willingly agree by saying, "Sure, what do you need?"

Jonathan knew David well enough to know that when he said, "Whatever you want me to do, I'll do it for you," David would not exceed the bounds of their relationship with his requests.

Perhaps an acrostic for FRIENDS might best explain how we know we have a Shanna–Sidney friendship.

F-*Faithful.* You don't have to wonder if tomorrow your friend will be there for you or not.

R-*Redeemed.* In any close relationships, we should not be unequally yoked.

I-*Interested.* In you. Not just in him or herself. Friendship travels on two-way streets.

E-*Eager.* Your cell phone rings. It's your friend. Is your response, "Oh, it's you"? Or is it, "Hey! Great to hear from you!"?

N-*Natural.* When you talk, can you be yourself? Do you feel like you're talking to a brother or sister?

D-*Discipler.* A true friend will help you grow stronger in your faith.

S-*Steady*. Dependable. There for you today and tomorrow. No matter what.

Friends. Who needs them? We all do because friends help us in our quest to live for Jesus, make an impact on our world, and honor our heavenly Father.

The Bible Addresses Friendship

"A friend loves at all times." (Proverbs 17:17)

"Wounds from a friend can be trusted." (Proverbs 27:6)

"Greater love has no one than this, that he lay down his life for his friends." (John 15:13)

Bernie Carbo

A Surprise Redemption

I have come that they may have life, and have it to the full.
—*John 10:10*

IF BERNIE CARBO HAD HIS WAY, HE'D BE DEAD
by now.

After all, he tried everything he could for the first fifteen years after he stopped playing major league baseball to make sure he didn't make it this far.

For one thing, he never stopped taking the dangerous drugs that he learned to take while playing for the Cincinnati Reds and Boston Red Sox. For another, the man who set up Carlton Fisk's famous body-English home run in Game Six of the 1975 World Series had nothing to live for.

That conclusion during the forty-fifth year of Bernie Carbo's life would have been a complete surprise to those who had watched his career and had enjoyed the go-for-broke way he played the game of baseball.

Carbo had broken into the major leagues in 1970 with a bang. Playing in the last home opener at ancient Crosley Field in Cincinnati on April 6, Carbo hit a home run in the fourth inning—part of a back-to-back-to-back trio of long balls by Lee May, Carbo, and Bobby Tolan. Carbo and the Reds won that game 5–1, handing George "Sparky" Anderson his first major league victory as a manager.

Carbo went on to hit .310 with 21 home runs in his debut season. *The Sporting News* named him their National League Rookie of the Year. Two seasons later, Cincinnati traded Carbo to the Boston Red Sox, thus setting in motion for the Detroit-born slugger a future showdown with his old team in one of the greatest games in baseball history.

It was October 21, 1975. The Reds and the Red Sox were locked up in a World Series showdown for the ages. Cincinnati held a 3–2 lead in games as the teams met at Fenway Park for Game Six. In the first inning, Fred Lynn hit a three-run home run to give Boston the lead. Cincinnati, however, caught and passed Boston to take a 6–3 lead into the bottom of the eighth inning. With two runners aboard in that inning, Bernie Carbo came up to the plate as a pinch hitter. He blasted a home run into left center field over the Green Monster to tie the game and keep the BoSox alive.

Nobody scored in the ninth, tenth, and eleventh innings.

In the last of the twelfth, future Hall of Fame catcher Carlton Fisk stood at the plate. He took a cut and hit a fly ball down the left field line. As Fisk started toward first, he turned toward the ball and waved with both arms—seemingly to coax the ball to stay fair. It did, hitting the foul pole for a game-winning home run.

That moment lives in baseball legend and TV replays as one of the most dramatic in baseball's long professional history. The fact that the Reds came back to win the series in the next game doesn't diminish the drama of Game Six and Bernie Carbo's key role in making it happen.

Seventeen years later, long after the cheering had stopped and Carbo had said good-bye to the majors after twelve seasons, 1,010 games, and 96 home runs, what was diminished was Bernie's will to live.

His marriage was over.

His mom had killed herself. His dad had died two months after that.

His drug problem raged.

He wanted to end the misery.

He needed hope, and he got it from two teammates who were unlikely resources—a man so odd he was called Spaceman and another man who had fought his own battle with illicit drugs.

When a person cries out for help—when a man is suicidal—it would not be expected that Bill "Spaceman" Lee and Ferguson Jenkins would save that man's life. And it would be even more unexpected that the actions of those two former big league pitchers would lead—indirectly, to be sure—to redemption through Jesus Christ for the man crying out for help.

If a man ever needed redemption it was Bernie Carbo.

When Carbo reached the end of his rope, he called on Lee and Jenkins, friends of his during his baseball days. They got him help. They made some phone calls and found a drug rehab institution in central Florida that would take Bernie in.

While in rehab, Carbo had an anxiety attack that was thought at first to be a heart attack. Doctors sent him to a Tampa hospital for treatment. While Carbo lay in his hospital bed, his roommate, a seventy-three-year-old former pastor, asked him some pointed questions.

"He asked me, 'Do you know God?'" Carbo recalls. "'Do you know Jesus Christ?'"

Carbo replied that his parents didn't believe in God, so he didn't know anything about Him or Jesus.

The elderly preacher persisted. He told Carbo, "You need to let your old self die. You need to be born again."

That message struck home with the struggling former baseball star. He took the old man at his word and prayed right there to trust Jesus Christ as his Savior.

The transformation was immediate. Carbo became an on-fire witness for Jesus Christ. Soon after he left the hospital and returned to the rehab center, a Christian psychologist took up where the evangelizing preacher left off. "God sent me to read the Bible to you," she told the newly reborn Carbo. For the next three months as Carbo edged toward getting back into society, she gave him his first lessons in living by biblical principles.

Scripture says that when a person has his sins forgiven through faith in Jesus Christ, he becomes a "new creation." Carbo became the poster boy for 2 Corinthians 5:17. No one who talked to Carbo could get very far into a conversation before he was enthusiastically talking about being reborn.

As soon as he got out of rehab, he and a friend began a Christian ministry called the Diamond Club, which was set up to tell "the greatest story ever told through the greatest game ever played."

Looking back on those dark December days in 1992, when he wanted to put the misery of life behind him yet was surprised by the joy that comes through faith in Christ, Carbo says, "Satan had his hands around my neck. He wanted to kill me. He won't ever do that again."

That's redemption!

If you ever get a chance to get an autograph from Carbo, you'll notice that along with his signature, he will scribble these words: "God is life."

For someone who so wanted death to end his existence not that many years ago, that's quite a statement. But after all, it's not a surprise, for Carbo himself expresses it best when he says, "I love Jesus because He has given me new life."

Looking Up

Bernie Carbo needed a shepherd. His life was on the outside of the sheep pen where wolves were about to devour him.

Jesus created a beautiful word picture of His rescue of us all in John 10:7–10. He described the pen where the sheep can find rest and protection, and He illustrated His own role by calling himself the "gate."

"I tell you the truth," Jesus told the Pharisees who were gathered to try to figure out just who this man was. "I am the gate for the sheep. All who ever came before me were thieves and robbers, but the sheep did not listen to them. I am the gate; whoever enters through me will be saved. He will come in and out, and find pasture. The thief comes only to steal and kill and destroy; I have come that they may have life, and have it to the full."

For Bernie, the thieves were the drugs and the despair and the lack of fulfillment that ate up his days. Those thieves had just about taken Carbo to his death—but then someone told him about the Shepherd—through whom comes safety and life and hope.

Have you met the Savior? Have you embraced the forgiveness that He alone can give because He alone was the perfect sacrifice for sin? Have you experienced the new life that has given Bernie Carbo and millions of other believers a reason to live life and live it to the full?

If not, listen again to the words of the old man: "You need to let your old self die. You need to be born again."

The Bible Addresses Redemption

"This righteousness from God comes through faith in Jesus Christ to all who believe. There is no difference, for all have sinned and fall short of the glory of God, and are justified freely by his grace through the redemption that came by Christ Jesus." (Romans 3:22–24)

"Christ redeemed us from the curse of the law by becoming a curse for us, for it is written, 'Cursed is everyone who is hung on a tree.'" (Galatians 3:13)

"In him we have redemption through his blood, the

forgiveness of sins, in accordance with the riches of God's grace." (Ephesians 1:7)

"For he has rescued us from the dominion of darkness and brought us into the kingdom of the Son he loves, in whom we have redemption, the forgiveness of sins." (Colossians 1:13–14)

"Christ Jesus came into the world to save sinners." (1 Timothy 1:15)

"We wait for . . . Jesus Christ, who gave himself for us to redeem us from all wickedness and to purify for himself a people that are his very own, eager to do what is good." (Titus 2:13–14)

16

Samkon Gado

A Humbling Experience

Clothe yourselves with humility.
—*1 Peter 5:5*

PERHAPS YOU SAW THE SIGNS BEGIN TO
sprout up at Lambeau Field during the middle of the Green Bay Packers'
forgettable season of 2005.

That was the year that Brett Favre struggled for the green and gold—
perhaps a season he wished he had not stuck around to play.

The Packers won just three football games that year, and Favre—lacking
the go-to receivers he had enjoyed in earlier seasons—threw twenty-nine
interceptions during the dismal season. There were few bright moments for
the Pack.

But amid the doldrums that marked those sixteen games, one ray of
light shined through—and thus the signs.

Perhaps the most popular were the ironic "In Gado We Trust" signs that
grabbed the attention of TV producers and made their way onto the small
screen during Green Bay games.

Ironic it was that a player who had so much trust in God would have
his name used as a play on words regarding the deity. The "Gado" of the
signs was a mighty mite sparkplug of a running back named Samkon
Gado—a scampering ball-carrier who ignited the Packers in a number of
late-season games with his surprising success.

That Samkon Gado played football for the Green Bay Packers in 2005
was surprising on several fronts.

Let's start with perhaps the most surprising aspect of his rise to the
NFL. See, Gado spent parts of the first nine years of his life in a land where
the letters NFL may have been better used as an acronym for No Food Left:
Nigeria. Seriously, when was the last time you heard, "At running back,
number 35, from Nigeria . . ."? Basketball scouts may scour Africa for the
next Luol Deng, but the mighty continent of Africa isn't exactly a hotbed of
pro football talent.

But there he was—Samkon (a name that in Tangale, his Nigerian dia-
lect, means *truth*) Gado (which means *inheritance*)—moving from being

released by the Kansas City Chiefs on October 4 to joining the Green Bay practice squad on October 19 to being listed on the roster on October 29 to earning a spot as the starting halfback on November 6 to being hailed a Green Bay hero shortly thereafter.

When Samkon was a crawling-around infant, his family moved from Nigeria to the United States so his dad could to go Wheaton College near Chicago. When Samkon was two years old, Jeremiah and Grace moved the family back across the ocean to Nigeria. Seven years later, they were back in the USA for good. The good of the NFL, obviously.

As to Gado's rise to instant fame with his success as a rookie runner for the Packers, nobody saw it coming.

Now, it's not a complete surprise that Liberty University, where Gado played his college football, produced an NFL player. It's happened on several occasions. Plus, Gado's head coach during his time with the Flames, Ken Karcher, was a former NFL quarterback. Still, this Division II-A school in the Big South Conference surely doesn't have a USC- or Michigan-type NFL pipeline.

Let's review. A kid grows up in Nigeria, moves to the United States, and attends Liberty University. That might be viewed as a road to the NFL if the kid ripped up the Big South, started forty games in his time in Lynchburg, led the nation in scoring or rushing or something—and then got drafted in the sixth round by somebody.

But that's not even close. Samkon Gado started a paltry three games for Liberty. And when he left Lynchburg, it wasn't in any way like the way his classmate and Lady Flames basketball star Katie Feenstra left. She was drafted in the first round by the WNBA in the spring of 2005. Gado was not drafted at all by the NFL.

Nigeria. Liberty. Three starts. Not drafted.

Hey, Sam! Welcome to grad school.

Not so fast. Remember, there was that connection between Coach Karcher and the NFL. Coach made a phone call to his old friend Dick Vermeil, who was heading into his final campaign as coach of the Kansas City Chiefs. Vermeil took a look at some film of Gado and invited him to training camp. He worked out with the Chiefs but was cut on August 29 after a mild neck injury kept him out of a preseason game. On September 5, the

Chiefs called him back in, but on October 4 they let him loose for the last time.

Maybe they didn't know it, but Green Bay had been looking him over. They had even scouted him when he was with the Chiefs. The Packers brought Gado in, he ran a 4.43 in the 40-yard dash, and they signed him up.

Within a matter of weeks, the youngster from Nigeria pretty much owned Lambeau Field.

To a football world that had OD'd on TO—feisty Terrell Owens—Gado brought something to the league that it needed: humility.

Ken Karcher noticed it when he was coaching Gado at Liberty. Karcher had wanted to redshirt Gado in 2004, but injuries forced him to play Gado—a move that cost Samkon development time as he moved toward his dream of playing in the NFL. But he didn't complain. Instead, as Karcher describes it, "he humbled himself," and he worked hard.

Gado's next coach noticed his humility as well. Mike Sherman, who gave Gado his big chance at the NFL, told the *Wisconsin State Journal,* "It is fun to be around someone with the humility he has." And this was after Gado had put together his biggest game: Three touchdowns and 103 yards on the ground against the Atlanta Falcons.

And what about Samkon himself? Does he understand the need for humility in a world where so many players are striving for attention? Indeed he does. "I believe it's in every person's nature," he said, "to be overcome with pride. If one is not careful, you could really get carried away."

But when Gado looks at how he ended up in the NFL, he's convinced that he's not the one who made it happen. When he looks back at the slim-to-none chance he had to stick with an NFL team, he says, "I say this is an act of God."

Samkon Gado's first-year NFL success was a surprise, but what would really be a surprise would be if this young man—whose favorite Bible verse is Joshua 1:9, which says, "Have I not commanded you? Be strong and courageous"—gets carried away with pride.

Looking Up

It is hard to be humble when you're good. Especially in sports.

Even athletes who are successful in high school soon learn to understand that they get treated special. Student A walks into the classroom having done all of her homework, having read the assignment, and prepared to discuss the subject in class. That's because the night before, she stayed home and worked hard. Student B walks into the classroom late. He kind of rushed through his homework in homeroom, flipped through the reading, and couldn't answer one question about the subject. That's because the night before, he was playing for the school's basketball team, and he scored 20 points.

So the two walk into the classroom, and guess who gets the attention. Guess who the teacher wants to talk to. Guess who gets all of the strokes and all of the compliments. Guess who gets ignored like a boring bulletin board.

We often build pride into people because we love sports so much.

If you are good at something—maybe you're like the girl with her homework done and you get a 4.0—it's tough to remember that it is God who gave you the ability. When we succeed in life, it is tough to deflect the attention to the One who made it possible.

But it's something we must do. The apostle Peter told us why. After he explained to his young readers that they should cover themselves with humility, he explained why. "God opposes the proud but gives grace to the humble" (1 Peter 5:5).

It's pretty simple. If we suck up all of the credit for our abilities and gifts, we are inviting God's disapproval. That, of course, will make life tough. But if we do as Samkon does and credit our maker for making us the way we are, God will bestow on us His grace. Peter goes on to say that God will even "lift you up."

How much better to let God do that than for us to try to lift ourselves up. That just leads to a big fall.

The Bible Addresses Humility

"Therefore, as God's chosen people, holy and dearly loved, clothe yourselves with compassion, kindness, humility." (Colossians 3:12)

"Be completely humble and gentle." (Ephesians 4:2)

"[God] guides the humble in what is right and teaches them his way." (Psalm 25:9)

"The fear of the Lord teaches a man wisdom, and humility comes before honor." (Proverbs 15:33)

Allyson Felix
A New Era of Morality
The requirements of the law are written on their hearts.
—Romans 2:15

ONE BY ONE THEY FELL BY THE WAYSIDE.

Perhaps most notoriously and embarrassingly, Ben Johnson and his gold medal crashed to the ground in a heap of ignominy. He had cruised effortlessly across the finish line at the Olympic Games in Seoul, Korea, running with the ease of a gazelle and with the power of a tiger. It was 1988, and Johnson had won the glamour race at the Olympics, the 100-meter dash. He had the world at his doorstep. He was on the cover of magazines. He was the athlete everyone wanted to talk to, touch, and be seen with.

Millions of dollars lay ahead for him in endorsements and myriad other opportunities.

And then came the announcement. He had cheated. When he ran that spellbinding race on the world's biggest stage, he was being pushed on by more than the nutrients from his latest meal and the muscles gained through hard work. He was on something.

Performance-enhancing drugs have pulled several top-name track athletes from the pedestals of fame and left them to wonder what they have done to their once-promising careers.

Ben Johnson. Tim Montgomery. Linford Christie. All prominent names turned into afterthoughts because they were afraid to depend on what God provided for them.

Then along comes Allyson Felix.

Allyson was just a normal teenager attending a little-known Christian high school in Southern California. At Los Angeles Baptist, she was just one of the girls. Then, as a freshman, she began racing past everyone in track meets. Before she had time to think about the implications, she had become one of the top prep runners in the country.

And then came the Olympics of 2002.

Suddenly she was not just a high school kid waiting for track season to get over so she could get a summer job at Disneyland. She was in Athens, Greece, standing next to the top 200-meter runners in the world—with the chance to beat them all.

And she almost did. In the biggest race of her young life—at age eighteen, she finished second in the 200 meters. In the finals at Athens, she was edged out for the gold medal by Veronica Campbell of Jamaica. Before she was twenty, Allyson had become the second-fastest 200-meter runner in the world.

Running had become something else besides a race for her. It had become a test. She was the new breed of runner. She was young and strong and standing on the precipice of fame. How would she respond?

Would young Allyson have her head turned by the promise offered by a vial of extra muscle she could inject into her already powerful body? Or would she stand her ground against artificiality? And if she did, why?

Even as a young runner, Miss Felix understood the reason for the questions. She knew that anyone who ran faster or jumped higher was subject to whispers about chemically enhanced performance. She also knew that she had something special she could bring to her sport—something she could bring only if she were to run her meets free of performance-enhancing drugs.

"My speed is a gift from God, and I run for His glory. My running is a gift from God. Having that support from God through hard practices and injuries makes all the difference. Whatever I do, it all comes from Him."

That might sound like "religious" talk to some people, but to the people who run the track and field world, it should sound like music. That statement, made by a maturing young woman, is more than God-talk. It is a declaration that can help restore the luster to a somewhat tarnished image for the sport, for Felix knows what's at stake.

"When people think of track," she said in *Sports Spectrum* magazine, "they think of scandal. Our sport is at a critical time. It's time to let track go in a new direction." And only the stars who depend solely on what "comes from [God]" can lead the way.

See, when an athlete truly wants to deflect the glory from herself and back onto God, she can dedicate herself to clean competition. "I always try to give God all the glory," Allyson says.

Keep an eye on this young lady. Her faith and her strength of character are on display, and she's ready for it. It's no made-up thing, for as she says,

"It's the standard I live up to every day. I would hope people would see that difference in me."

People are looking for athletes to restore and maintain integrity in the sport of track and field. They will definitely see the difference a life dedicated to God and godly living can make.

Looking Up

It's rather hard to have a good testimony for Jesus Christ when you're on drugs. That sounds like a pretty obvious point, but it's not like it hasn't been tried.

In the 1980s, there was a major league baseball player who spoke in interviews about his faith in Jesus Christ. But then he got busted for drug abuse and was kicked out of baseball.

Then he came back on the scene, proclaiming again that he wanted to be a witness for Christ.

And then he got busted again.

In all, he was nicked for failing drug tests something like eight times.

Although the Bible does not address the misuse of drugs specifically, it is safe to say that there are verses that address the related issue. One is Ephesians 5:18, which says, "Do not get drunk on wine, which leads to debauchery. Instead, be filled with the Spirit." Sure, drugs and wine are not the same thing, but they have the same effect.

Allyson's words regarding her talent in track could be used as an explanation for this verse in relation to using stimulants of any kind. She said, "Whatever I do, it all comes from within." When a person is filled with the Holy Spirit, He is the influence, and there is no need for an outside influence such as drugs or alcohol.

There's another verse that we can hang on to for help with this question of the use of drugs or alcohol. Proverbs 21:17 says, "He who loves pleasure will become poor; whoever loves wine and oil will never be rich." Again, our dedication and our allegiance must be to God and His standards, not to some stimulant.

This is just one part of the total moral picture that we are attempting to paint with our lives.

The Bible Addresses Morality and Care for the Body

"But just as he who called you is holy, so be holy in all you do." (1 Peter 1:15)

"My son, pay attention to what I say; listen closely to my words. Do not let them out of your sight, keep them within your heart; for they are life to those who find them and health to a man's whole body." (Proverbs 4: 20–22)

"For the kingdom of God is not a matter of eating and drinking, but of righteousness, peace and joy in the Holy Spirit." (Romans 14:17)

18

Mike Maroth

Dependability

Simply let your "Yes" be "Yes."
—Matthew 5:37

LET'S START WITH WHAT MIGHT BE A startling
revelation. Pro athletes—even Christian pro athletes—are not always
dependable.

Over the years that I've been interviewing pro athletes for *Sports Spectrum* magazine and for books I've written, I've experienced several instances
when brothers in Christ missed scheduled appointments, told what appeared
to be "truth shading" to avoid being interviewed, or just flat-out went back
on their word.

Sometimes it goes like this: "Hi, I'm from *Sports Spectrum* magazine.
Can I get just a few minutes with you? We'd like to let you tell your story of
faith."

"Oh, okay. But I'm kinda busy right now getting ready for batting practice. How about after the game?"

So I go to the press box to go over my questions and check my tape
recorder to make sure it's working (and watch a little baseball). After the
game, as soon as I'm allowed back into the locker room, I go in. But by
then, the object of my attention has showered and high-tailed it out of the
clubhouse. Undependable.

This happens regularly: The player's agent calls and tells me that the
player has agreed to an interview. He'll be calling at about two-thirty, the
agent says. Two-thirty comes and goes quietly away. Two fifty. Three o'clock.
By then, I know the drill. It's not going to happen. Undependable.

That's why Mike Maroth's story is so appealing. He answers his e-mail.
He responds to interview requests. And on the biggest day of his young
career as a pitcher, he followed through on a promise—despite a major
change in his situation.

On Monday, June 3, 2002, Mike Maroth was a minor league pitcher in
the Detroit Tigers organization. He was pitching for the Toledo Mud Hens
in the International League.

The producers of *Sports Spectrum* radio heard that Maroth was a solid

Christian, and they wanted to interview him for the program. So after finding out about Mike's faith, the SS Radio people called the Toledo PR people on that Monday. They talked to Maroth, and he agreed to be on the radio program on June 8. He would go one-on-one with *Sports Spectrum* host Chuck Swirsky, who was also the play-by-play announcer for the Toronto Raptors in the NBA. The subject that day would be minor league baseball and Mike's walk with Jesus Christ.

On Friday, June 7, everything changed for Maroth. He got the call he had been waiting for since he was drafted out of Central Florida University. The Detroit Tigers wanted him to be in Detroit on Saturday. And he was not just driving up to Motown to model the Tigers' Old English *D*. He had been tabbed as the starting pitcher for the Tigers in their Saturday night game at Comerica Park against the Philadelphia Phillies in an interleague contest.

That meant that on Saturday, June 8, when he was scheduled to be doing a live radio interview, he was also slated to be getting mentally ready to take the mound for the very first time as a major league pitcher.

For the *Sports Spectrum* radio staff, this was a disappointment waiting to happen. So they prepared themselves for Plan B. Knowing what a big day this was for Maroth and knowing how seriously professional athletes take the concept of focusing on the task ahead, they figured they would be filling that twelve-minute slot with alternative programming.

So when the designated time came when Mike was supposed to call in, they sat nervously by the phone. Would the just-about-to-become major league rookie come through, or would he take the route so many others have taken and use his situation as an excuse not to do the interview?

Here's what the *Sports Spectrum* radio audience heard from Swirsky that day. "Welcome back to *Sports Spectrum*. This is Chuck Swirsky, joined by Mike Maroth of the Detroit Tigers. Mike, thanks for picking up the phone. We appreciate it."

"Mike Maroth of the Detroit Tigers." Imagine how good that sounded to the young lefthander as he began the interview. He had come through with his commitment, and he was being announced to a national listenership as "Mike Maroth of the Detroit Tigers."

That, Mike told Chuck, was "a dream come true."

As the interview progressed, Mike's dependability was rewarded in a surprising way. On the program, listeners can call in and ask questions of the athlete being interviewed.

Midway through the interview, this exchange took place.

Swirsky: "We've only a couple of minutes remaining, but we've got a special call on the line, and we understand his name is Luke. So Luke, we've not set this up, and by the way, Mike, I have no idea who this is. But go ahead, Luke, you're on with Mike Maroth."

Luke: "Mike, that has a nice ring to it: Mike Maroth of the Detroit Tigers. It sounds a lot better than Toledo. I'm the scout who drafted Mike in the third round of the draft back in 1998. I was working as a scout for the Boston Red Sox, and now I'm with the Arizona Diamondbacks. But you know what? I'm a Detroit Tiger fan now. Once a scout signs a player, they hope and pray that he'll make it to the major leagues. And Mike has made the big step to the majors. I'm really proud of him. I pray about the players I get in the draft—the ones God wants me to have, not necessarily the ones I think I ought to have. And the Lord has blessed me by giving me the players I need to have. When I get a player like Mike to play in the big leagues—well, he's a good Christian and it makes it all the better."

On this day, with listeners on 230 radio stations listening in, Mike Maroth and the scout who talked the Red Sox into drafting him, were reunited and could enjoy—at least by phone—Mike's big day. Seems like a pretty good tradeoff for keeping his commitment.

Also in the course of the interview, Chuck complimented Maroth for keeping his commitment to the radio program, to which Maroth responded, "I just pray and try to stay focused. I'm not going to change anything. Obviously, God has me here for a purpose, and He's blessed me with this ability."

In the years since Maroth did that radio interview on the day of his first major league game—which he won, by the way, with an outstanding outing against the Phillies—he has proved that his first-day dependability was not a fluke. He continues to be accessible, dependable, and godly in his approach to life in the major leagues.

In fact, he and his wife were honored in 2004 with the Bill Emerson Good Samaritan Award for their work in Detroit with those who don't have enough to eat. Mike and Brooke contacted Rock and Wrap It Up, a national organization that takes extra food from concert venues and donates it to local soup kitchens. Their idea was to take food that was not used by the teams in the clubhouses at Comerica Park and make it available to those in need. It was just more evidence that Maroth takes his calling as a Christian seriously and that he is one of the most dependable athletes you'd want to meet.

Think of how comfortable dependable people make us feel. When someone is expected to do something and he or she comes through, the feeling left behind is calming and refreshing. Contrast that with how we feel when someone lets us down after promising to come through. Betrayal. Anger. Disappointment.

This concept is wonderfully explained in Proverbs: "Like the coolness of snow at harvest time is a trustworthy messenger to those who send him; he refreshes the spirit of his masters" (25:13).

Looking Up

On the day Mike Maroth got to the majors, he had an opportunity that most of us will never have. He had the chance to tell people across the country on more than two hundred radio stations about his relationship with Jesus Christ.

He had no idea when he answered those questions on *Sports Spectrum* radio who might be out there listening—who might be willing to listen to what he had to say about the gospel simply because of his status as a major leaguer. Perhaps he was even able to lead someone to Christ that day.

None of us know, when an opportunity arises, what effect our words or actions might have on others. Our task is not to try to figure the result or impact of what we say or do, but to live and speak in a way that God can use for His glory.

It's a servant mentality, which Maroth describes by saying, "Jesus was a servant, and He tells us to be servants ourselves. All I am trying to do is serve others."

Is that our goal? Are we dependable in our servanthood—looking out for the good of those we serve rather than protecting our own situation?

The Bible Addresses Dependability

"His master replied, 'Well done, good and faithful servant! You have been faithful with a few things; I will put you in charge of many things." (Matthew 25:23)

"Whoever can be trusted with very little can also be trusted with much." (Luke 16:10)

"But as for you, continue in what you have learned and have become convinced of." (2 Timothy 3:14)

"Be on your guard; stand firm in the faith; be men of courage; be strong." (1 Corinthians 16:13)

19

Dany Heatley

Unreal Forgiveness

Be kind and compassionate to one another, forgiving each other,
just as in Christ God forgave you.
—*Ephesians 4:32*

DANY HEATLEY COULD HAVE GONE TO prison. Instead, he went to the Olympics.

Dan Snyder's family could have gone for the jugular. Instead, they went for forgiveness.

The names of Dany Heatley and Dan Snyder will forever be etched together in NHL history. In September 2003, the two were teammates on the Atlanta Thrashers hockey team. Two young men who grew up loving hockey—thrust together through the nuances of signings and draft picks and trades to wear the same NHL sweaters.

They became more than teammates; they became friends. A young hockey player who grew up in Germany and was a first-round draft pick in 2000 after playing at the University of Wisconsin, and a young man from Elmira, Ontario, who entered the NHL as an undrafted free agent in 1999.

Their friendship transcended hockey, as Dan Snyder's brother would later say: "My brother talked about Dany constantly. Dany was so special to my brother."

So it was that in September 2003, the two hockey players got into Dany Heatley's Ferrari for an early fall drive through some rural roads near Atlanta. Who knows what caused him to decide to test fate that day and drive his car at speeds better suited for the Atlanta Speedway than for the Georgia countryside. And who knows what caused this young man with great reflexes to lose control of his prized car with his best friend seated in the passenger seat.

Both hockey players were seriously injured when the Ferrari flew off the road and crashed. But as so often happens, the driver survived. The passenger—the innocent party—did not. Head injuries put Dan Snyder in a coma and in just a few days' time claimed his life.

The hockey world braced for the expected outcome. A bereaved family, deprived of their son because of another pro athlete who didn't know how to control his impulses, could have set themselves up for life and taken down a recovering Dany Heatley.

They could have gone after his life and put it on hold in a jail somewhere—effectively ending his hockey career. After all, it was his negligence that had ended not only their son's promising career but his promising life as well.

Graham Snyder and his family could have thrown the book at the man who killed their son. And who could blame them? They have to spend the rest of their lives with the gnawing, unrelenting pain of Dan's death. They look every day at his picture while knowing that never again would they hear his voice or feel the hug of his strong arms. Their dreams shattered, they could easily have shattered Dany Heatley's life too.

But there was something that stopped Graham Snyder and his family from doing that. Something called faith. Something they learned as a strong Christian family steeped in the Mennonite tradition.

"This has been a tragedy and we've lost our son," Snyder told the *Atlanta Journal-Constitution.* "But to lose another person would be senseless." To their way of thinking, prosecuting Heatley would only cause more pain to a young man who knew full well what he had done and would have to live the rest of his life with the consequences.

And it wasn't just that Graham Snyder was going to let the chance to stick it to Dany in court pass by. He decided that the family would be active in helping him—"by doing everything we can" for Heatley, as Dan's dad put it. He figured that one family's tragedy couldn't be softened by causing another family to suffer. "We want him to know he's forgiven," the elder Snyder proclaimed.

Although he could have asked a judge to go after Heatley on a charge of vehicular homicide, Graham Snyder didn't. Instead, he asked the judge not to send Heatley to jail. The judge didn't—he sentenced Heatley to serve three years' probation and make 150 speeches about how dangerous it is to drive too fast.

The Snyders discovered something important about forgiveness. It lets life go on. Blaming, accusing, finger-pointing—those all stop life in its tracks and bury people under the rubble of pain. Forgiveness, Graham Snyder said, helped his family "move on."

"We are all human beings, and we know that humans make mistakes," Graham Snyder said in a statement after the funeral service. "We want you to know that we do not lay blame on Dany Heatley for the accident that took our son from us. . . ." There is nothing to gain from harboring resentment or anger toward others.

In 2005, Dany Heatley left the Atlanta Thrashers behind and moved on to the Ottawa Senators. In 2006, he suited up for the Canadian Olympic hockey team. Those events, just as the Snyders' magnanimous gesture of forgiveness, helped Heatley heal from the daily, gnawing regret for his part in the accident that took his friend. In court, he had told the Snyders, "The mistake I made that night will be a mistake that will stay with me the rest of my life."

Looking Up

Hyperbole?

Is that what Jesus was using when Peter asked Him how many times he should forgive someone? Peter figured he had it covered when he suggested that he would forgive seven times. But Jesus surprised the man He called Rock by telling him it took seventy-seven times to forgive.

Was He kidding? Was He exaggerating for emphasis?

Well, not exactly. What Christ was doing was referring all the way back to Genesis in the Torah to something Lamech said in chapter 4, verse 24: "If Cain is avenged seven times, then Lamech seventy-seven times."

This repetition of sevens seems to be indicative of the concept of never ending. In other words, our forgiveness is not to be considered done because we say a meek "I'm sorry." Our forgiveness is to extend indefinitely into the future.

Take a look at the story Jesus shared after He told Peter that forgiveness knows no limit. He told about a servant who had a debt that was too much for him to pay. So he threw himself on the mercy of the master and begged for forgiveness. The master acquiesced and forgave the debt.

Subsequently, the servant discovered that someone owed him an amount equaling a small fraction of his debt to the master. Did he forgive that tiny debt? No, he had the poor guy tossed into prison.

He must not have gotten word about the seventy-seven times of forgiveness; he wouldn't even forgive once.

That awful creature is what we are when we fail to forgive, Jesus says.

How much better it would be for us to use a little hyperbole in our forgiveness—forgiving more times than we have to instead of holding back on the forgiveness we need to bestow on others.

It's one more way of looking up to the Father and thanking Him for the forgiveness He lavished on us.

The Bible Addresses Forgiveness

"Do not repay anyone evil for evil. Be careful to do what is right in the eyes of everybody." (Romans 12:17)

"Bear with one another and forgive whatever grievances you have against one another." (Colossians 3:13)

Dwight Howard

A Testament of Effort

Lazy hands make a man poor, but diligent hands bring wealth.
—*Proverbs 10:4*

HOW WOULD YOU LIKE TO BE SET FOR LIFE AT age eighteen?

That question is one of the dilemmas that extremely talented athletes face as they decide how they are going to live. One day you're a high school senior trying to scare up enough money to take your girlfriend to a decent restaurant. Then the NBA draft rolls around, your name is called, you sign on the dotted line—and you can buy the restaurant. Cash.

You're barely old enough to vote. You've just barely escaped the restrictions of the graduated driver's license. Your high school diploma still smells like new.

And you've got a contract in your hands that will pay you somewhere between $11 and $13 million over the next few years. By the time you are old enough to vote for the president of the United States, you'll have made more money than he'll make if he were president for the next twenty-seven years.

So now what do you do? You're richer than just about everybody, and you haven't really done anything yet. How are you going to handle that?

If you're Dwight Howard, you're going to work. You're going to work very, very hard.

When Dwight Howard was young—no, really young, like in the eighth grade—he wrote in his journal that he wanted to be the number one pick in the NBA draft. Then he went about making it happen. It didn't hurt that he hit a growth explosion a year or so later that turned him from a six-foot-two guard into a six-foot-eleven power broker. But he also put forth a huge amount of effort to make his dream come true.

He also went against the grain regarding schooling. Since kindergarten, Dwight had gone to Southwestern Atlanta Christian Academy. This is not quite DeMatha, the famed high school basketball powerhouse. It was certainly no breeding ground for future NBA players. But his family kept him in a school whose gym could seat barely five hundred people and whose student population hovered around three hundred.

Yet Howard was driven. Driven by his dreams and driven by his desire to use his ability to spread the message of Jesus Christ in the NBA. He made that clear even before he was drafted, saying that one of the reasons he was joining the NBA was to let others know about his faith.

But just signing a contract for mega-millions and showing up in a slick NBA uniform won't build a kid much of a platform. And Howard knew that.

He would have to take advantage of his selection, and he would have to turn his career into something special. He knows that to garner the attention he wants for his story of faith, he has to be very, very good. In fact, he has stated, "I want to be the best basketball player." Not the best he can be. The best.

And right away he began to show that he knows how to do that: Through hard work. He said, "I'm going to keep working at it every day. God has blessed me with a lot of talent. I have to use it the right way."

The kid was working hard even before David Stern stood before the cameras and said, "With the first pick in the 2004 NBA draft, the Orlando Magic selects Dwight Howard of Southwestern Atlanta Christian Academy." Howard would wake up at 5:00 A.M. to shoot baskets at the high school gym. No scouts were there. No NBA execs. Just Dwight, a basketball, and his desire to get better.

Once Howard put on the blue and white number 12 uniform of the Magic, he demonstrated that he was in the NBA to work. In his first season in the league, he played in all eighty-two games for Orlando. He led the team in both blocked shots and rebounds. And he was so impressive that many felt he was on the verge of becoming one of the top players in the game.

Some people think they know hard work when they see it. They head for the gym, take fifty jump shots, kind of sprint up and down the court a couple of times, do a few push-ups, and head for the showers. They mistake the word *work* for *shirk*. What they need is somebody a lot older and wiser and hard-nosed to teach them what work means.

Howard has had those people. First, of course, was his dad, Dwight Sr. A Georgia state trooper and the athletic director at Southwestern Atlanta

Christian, Big Dwight was there to show his son the value of sweat equity. Second is Pat Williams, longtime executive for the Magic. He says, "The most important thing Dwight has to do is to outwork everybody in this business and take his game to the next level." If he does put in the work, Williams feels, he'll have a great platform from which to share his faith in Jesus Christ.

And then there is Clifford Ray. Thirty-seven years Dwight's senior, old Cliff is a former professional basketball player from back in the day when you'd make in a year what young Dwight draws in interest. In a month.

But there he is on the court. Sweating. Puffing. Cajoling. Pushing. Trying to show young Dwight the moves he'll need to battle Shaquille and the fellows.

Ray is just what Howard needs—a catalyst to take his willingness to work hard and to help hone his skills to match his prodigious potential. Not afraid to challenge the young superstar-in-the-making, Ray toughens Howard for the rigors of NBA board battles.

But beyond the people, Dwight Howard has a verse—a Scripture that he feels best details why he is willing to work so hard despite the fact that he's incredibly wealthy whether he puts in the extra effort or not.

"James 2:26 says that faith without works is dead. That's my favorite Scripture. I use it during the basketball season. You can talk about it. You can write it down. But if you don't do it, you're not going to get all God has for you.

"A lot of people didn't think that Dwight Howard, a kid from Southwestern Christian Academy, could go straight to the NBA. I wrote it down, and then I put the work in."

Looks like the Magic knew what they were doing when they grabbed Dwight Howard.

Looking Up

How would you react to: "Good morning, folks. Thanks for coming to church. You know, I didn't really feel like putting together a message this week, so I decided just to talk to you about whatever comes to mind. Let's see, I'm going to open my Bible and wherever my finger lands, I'm going to read that passage."

Or how about this: "Hello, sir. I'm here to install your carpet. I didn't feel like bringing all that stretching stuff with me today, and I didn't bother to pick up any of those nasty carpet tack strips, so I'm just going to lay the stuff down, fire a couple of nails into in, and call it good. Okay?"

We would not stand for either situation. Lazy people simply don't get the job done—at church or on the job. Or on the basketball court.

We don't like to see laziness in others, so we should not demonstrate it in the things we do.

There's nothing wrong with resting. God rested—but only after six days of hard work, and after He had finished what He had set out to do.

Colossians 3:23 tells us that whatever we do, we must work at it with all of our strength. It seems that Paul is telling us that even in our secular work—our day-to-day labor, whether in school or on a job—we must be diligent, keeping in mind that God is watching and expecting us to give life our all. Additionally, hard work results in respect from others, as 1 Thessalonians 5:12 suggests.

And then there is spiritual work. In Philippians 2:12, Paul said we must "work out [our] salvation," which simply means that we have some spiritual growing to do as Christians, and that takes spiritual discipline.

Work. It's not a dirty word. It's not a result of the curse. It is what God expects of each of us if we are to be testifying image-bearers of the One who has worked so hard on our behalf.

The Bible Addresses Hard Work

"For you yourselves know how you ought to follow our example. We were not idle when we were with you." (2 Thessalonians 3:7)

"Make it your ambition to lead a quiet life, to mind your own business and to work with your hands, just as we told you, so that your daily life may win the respect of outsiders." (1 Thessalonians 4:11–12)

"Whatever you do, work at it with all your heart, as working for the Lord, not for men." (Colossians 3:23)

Albert Pujols
Please Pray

The Lord is near to all who call on him, to all who call on him in truth.
—Psalm 145:18

ONCE YOU'VE SEEN ALBERT PUJOLS STAND
at home plate with a stick of lumber in his hand and smack a hunk of
horsehide far into the night, prayer might indeed be something that comes
to mind.

A prayer not for Mr. Pujols but for the poor pitcher who might need a
little divine protection.

Yet it is the mighty Albert who wants prayer.

Let's begin by looking at what this young man did in his first five years
in the major leagues.

He hit 201 home runs. He knocked in 621 runs. He batted .332. To
understand what that means in the bigger context of baseball history, consider the stats of a slugger by the name of Joe DiMaggio. Just in case you
don't know, DiMaggio is considered one of the greatest hitters in the history
of the nearly 140 years of professional baseball in North America. Some
would put him at the top. Here's what his stats looked like after five seasons:

He hit 168 home runs. He knocked in 591 runs. He batted .343.

Notice any similarities?

Albert Pujols does not just stroke lazy singles to left. The man murders
the baseball.

Former Pittsburgh Pirates manager Lloyd McClendon said of Albert,
"I've never seen anything like it. No situation seems to rattle him." A teammate for a while, Fernando Vena said of Pujols, "He's a freak. There's no
awe in his eyes."

This man hits baseballs as hard as anybody but Barry Bonds—and
nobody's ever seen a ball hit harder than Bonds did in his prime.

So think about Albert Pujols at the plate—standing a scant sixty feet, six
inches away from the pitcher. And once the pitcher releases the pitch, he's
perhaps six feet closer to Pujols and his mighty swing. Think about that and
then ask who needs prayer.

Yes, Albert says he does.

It's not that Pujols doesn't believe in his ability. He's not stupid. He knows how good he is. But he also knows that with that ability comes a huge responsibility. And he knows that while he's grown to become an icon of power and talent in the majors, he's got a lot of growing to do spiritually.

"I'm still a baby in Christ," Pujols said before he began his fifth major league season. "I keep learning and just follow my leader—follow the things the Lord wants me to do."

One of those things was to start, along with his wife Deidre, the Pujols Family Foundation. They felt that one of the best ways to follow God's leading was to help others. With the Foundation, two of the specific needs the Pujols meet are with children with Down syndrome and with a school that they support in the Dominican Republic.

Also, Pujols is involved with an organization in St. Louis that each summer puts together a Christian Family Day at the ballpark. Pujols works with the organizer, Judy Boen, to get fans to attend a Cardinals game and then listen to Pujols and other Christians on the team as they give their testimonies.

Those two activities—the Foundation and the Christian Family Day—are just two of the reasons Albert Pujols wants people to pray for him.

In case you haven't been following professional sports very closely, this is highly unusual. Think about it for a few minutes. When was the last time you heard or read about a pro athlete—especially one who makes more money than just about everybody but Bill Gates—asking people to pray for him?

Seriously, think about it. Football? Hockey? Basketball? Soccer? Golf? Donovan? Sidney? Tracy? Freddy? Annika?

These people are rich and famous. Their needs outside of continuing to perform on the field or course or court seem to be few. Prayer? Those who face them might need it, that's for sure. But to hear them ask for it?

Unlikely.

So up steps Albert Pujols, smacker of prodigious home runs. Holder of the National League MVP trophy for 2005. Centerpiece of one of the best teams in baseball.

"Pray for me," he says.

See, Albert Pujols is one of those rare top-of-the-line athletes who understands that life is not all ground balls, line drives, and grand slam home runs. Life is about having a wife to honor and having a family to take care of. Life is about having a church to attend. It's about having an obligation to help others in a manner that corresponds to God's blessings.

So here's what Pujols wants fans to pray about:

"Pray that I don't fall into temptation. The devil wants to go get you out there any time you try to do great things for our Lord."

Mr. Pujols, in a sense, has a target on his back. Like another former St. Louis sports star, Kurt Warner, Pujols is not ashamed to talk about his faith in Jesus Christ. He speaks openly and often about spiritual matters, so much so that many sports fans know him now as not just a strong hitter but also a strong Christian. Therefore, should he falter in any way, should he indeed fall to temptation, the fall would be loud.

We recall what happened at a late 1990s Super Bowl when another strong Christian succumbed to temptation the night before the big game. His name, which it would do no good to use here, is still mentioned by skeptical writers who want to dismiss the whole Christian thing by pointing accusing fingers at one fallen brother.

So Albert unabashedly asks for people to pray for purity and freedom from the pitfalls of temptation.

But what else does the hammerin' first baseman want us to pray for?

"Pray that I would keep my eyes on Jesus and stay humble."

For anyone who ever hit a home run, sank a long putt, kicked a field goal, hit a three-pointer, or even put a puck past a goalie, humility is a problem.

Yet imagine hitting more than fifty home runs in a season. Imagine making millions of dollars every year. Imagine driving any car you want. Imagine being told you are as good as Joe DiMaggio. Imagine knowing that for the rest of your life you will never have to work. And you're not yet thirty.

Then try to be humble. Try to figure that you're not better than the guy in row Y, seat 13, who makes deliveries for an auto parts store and drives a 1993 Toyota.

No wonder Albert wants people to pray for him.

It helps to have people around him like Rick Horton, St. Louis

Cardinals team chaplain. "He's just a sinner saved by grace like the rest of us," says Horton, who had his own taste of being a major leaguer. Horton says that when Pujols first began speaking up and speaking out as a Christian in front of groups, he had this message: "I'm just trying to grow in my relationship with the Lord. That's the most important thing in my life, and I'm just trying to understand who He is more every day."

When everybody thinks you're the man, and you think the Man is Jesus, then staying humble gets a whole lot easier.

And one more thing Albert Pujols prays about.

"Pray for wisdom in every financial decision."

See, when you have money coming in like most of us have water—flowing in unstopping portions—you need a different kind of wisdom. We may need help knowing how to get gas money to get to our job at Starbucks. Albert needs help in making sure he doesn't let money overwhelm him and stop him from being someone God can use. That's why he and his wife started the Pujols Family Foundation—to see how they could use some of their money to help others.

Albert Pujols is a student of the game of baseball. He studies pitchers and he studies situations to see how he can get better. But he is also a student of his faith. He studies the Word and he seeks ways he can improve his walk with Jesus Christ. And one of the key ways he does it is through prayer.

Watch him play and you'll see a professional at work—one of the best ever.

Watch him pray, and you'll see a role model for each of us in learning how to lean on God and worship Him with our lives.

Then pray for Albert Pujols. And if you're a pitcher, duck.

Looking Up

God is omniscient. He knows everything.

God is sovereign. He has everything under control.

He is the Alpha and the Omega—the beginning and the end.

Then why pray? If God already knows and if God already has things planned and if God knows the beginning from the end—then why do we bow our heads and earnestly tell Him what is on our hearts?

As Christian comedian Mark Lowry once said, "Has it ever occurred to you that nothing ever occurs to God?" We don't surprise God by our prayers, but we honor Him.

See, Jesus taught us to pray. And Jesus commanded us to pray.

How ridiculous it would be for our Savior to teach us and tell us to do something that would do no good.

Jesus himself set the example in John 17 when He prayed a long and detailed prayer to the Father. In that prayer, He prayed for the people who were within earshot of Him, but incredibly He prayed for us. He said, "My prayer is not for them [His contemporary followers] alone. I pray also for those who will believe in me through their message" (v. 20). That's us.

He prayed for our witness to a wondering world.

He prayed for unity of believers.

He prayed for our future presence in glory with Him.

Sometimes we can think too much. We can talk ourselves out of the most awesome privilege known to man: Talking directly to the God of the universe.

May Albert Pujols' call to prayer remind us that the *subject* of our prayer is not as important as the *act* of our prayer. Prayer is obedience to the Father, and it is just one more way we tell Him how much we love, trust, and honor Him.

The Bible Addresses Prayer

"If my people, who are called by my name, will humble themselves and pray and seek my face and turn from their wicked ways, then will I hear from heaven." (2 Chronicles 7:14)

"Because he turned his ear to me, I will call on him as long as I live." (Psalm 116:2)

"If you believe, you will receive whatever you ask for in prayer." (Matthew 21:22)

"Be joyful in hope, patient in affliction, faithful in prayer." (Romans 12:12)

"Pray continually." (1 Thessalonians 5:17)

22

Teri MacDonald-Cadieux
Leaning on God

*Lean not on your own understanding; in all your ways acknowledge him,
and he will make your paths straight.*
—*Proverbs 3:5*

MOST OF US CAN RATTLE OFF THE NAMES OF
famous people who have suffered severe neck injuries that have changed
their lives—or even taken their lives.

Joni Eareckson Tada.

Christopher Reeve.

Dale Earnhardt.

But race car driver and executive and all-around racing maven Teri
MacDonald-Cadieux can go a step further than just naming names. She can
tell you exactly which vertebra each of those people broke, and she can tell
you what it means to break one of those key bones in the neck.

C–1: That's the break that cost Dale Earnhardt his life, she will recall.

C–3 and C–4: Those are the neck bones that put Joni Eareckson in a
wheelchair at age seventeen.

C–3: That's what made Christopher Reeve, Superman, helpless and
eventually lose his life.

And C–2. Well, according to Teri MacDonald-Cadieux, breaking that
will give you a mortality rate of 96 percent. Only 4 percent of people who
crack that bone live. And then most of them are paralyzed.

So what's the deal? Is this lady a doctor or something?

No, Teri is up on all these things because she too found herself with a
doctor who looked up from the X rays of her neck and said, "Yes, it's broken."

Her injury was of the C–2 variety—the dead-almost-every-time kind—
and she had not one, not two, but three breaks in there.

It happened in 1997 while Teri was racing her car on a road track in
Gainesville, Georgia. On the course was a tricky corner that had drivers staring at a bridge abutment as they scooted their cars through the turn. If you
played it just right and turned your car just as it should be turned, she
recalls, the abutment was not a big deal. You just had to plan ahead, steer

properly going into the turn, and you were past it.

Over and over she maneuvered her car past the nasty abutment.

But one time, as she was tooling around the course at 150 miles an hour—third from the front and just biding her time for a later run at the lead—a fourth driver decided that he wanted in on the top-four action. So he tried to move around Teri into third place—just as the lead cars were heading for that dangerous curve and the looming abutment.

As he jockeyed for position, he tapped the rear end of Teri's race car. Traveling at more than twice expressway speed, Teri lost control as her car lost its grip on the track. Her automobile slid sideways into that abutment, and her car rolled anywhere from six to eight times. Her seat gave way, and she ended up tangled in the rear of the car, underneath the roll bar.

When rescuers got to what was left of Teri's car, they dug through the twisted metal to get to her. Their first reaction upon seeing her was surprise.

"It's a girl!" they exclaimed.

And, as Teri describes it, they tried to handle her gently as they extracted her from her ride. "If it had been a guy, they would have just grabbed him and dragged him out of there. But with me, they were more gentle."

It's a good thing, because although no one seemed to notice for a while, she had a broken neck.

When she was taken to the hospital, the doctors X-rayed her, looked over the film, and sent her on her way. No breaks. No problem. Go home.

A little later, though, another radiologist took a look at the X rays and came to a different conclusion. A quick phone call changed things for Teri.

"You'd better get back in here. You have a broken neck."

It was the C–2 vertebra—the one that is a 96-percent death sentence—cracked in three places.

Before she could ask any questions, they slapped a halo brace on her neck, screwed it down, and started talking about thirteen weeks of rehab followed by eight more, and then they would assess the situation.

Enter Dad MacDonald. And enter a family leaning on God.

"My father was with my brother, who was running Winston Cup at Martinsville. My husband was testing with the Andrettis in Pennsylvania. He got there as soon as possible.

"And they began praying."

But they didn't just keep it in the family. Prayer chains sprang up to pray for Teri. Twenty-four-hour prayer chains were set up. As Teri now says, "We called every Christian and every church we knew.

"My father called everybody and just said, 'Pray, pray, pray.'"

Teri has developed her own illustration of what prayer can be in our lives—three stages or perhaps pictures of prayer.

"Your prayer life is like one of three things," she begins. "Prayer could be like a spare tire. You know it's back there, and you can use it if needed. Or it could be like climate control. When life gets hot, you ask Jesus to crank up the air. Or it could be like a steering wheel: your hands are always on it. You are always connected to God through your prayer life."

As Teri looks back, she knows what her prayer life became.

"I started praying," she recalls. "My prayer life went from the spare tire to the steering wheel. I started praying—and all those other people started praying, and God did a miraculous thing."

All that leaning on God paid off.

"It was not thirteen weeks with the halo. It was five weeks," she says. "I flew to Miami. The screws came out of my head. The body cast came off. And I was fine. I wore the Miami J collar for four weeks. Because of the power of God, I was back driving twelve weeks after rolling my car and breaking my neck."

No wonder Teri MacDonald calls herself "a walking miracle."

Looking Up

Depending on God is not easy. It may sound like an easy thing to do, but in order to hand ourselves over to Him and allow His will to be done, we have to take a huge step. It means we have to trust God that He knows what He is doing.

What if Teri had said, "Look, God. You didn't have to allow that guy to bang into my bumper and send me into that wall. How can I trust you when you allowed that to happen?" Trust in God means that we hand everything over to Him and allow Him to work as He desires.

Step one in doing that is putting God on the throne of our lives.

Teri MacDonald-Cadieux struggled with that—even after the accident.

But a conversation she says she had with God helped her reestablish God as in charge of her life.

"God asked me, 'What do you love more than anything?'" she says. Then she felt that He was running through a checklist of options:

"When you watch TV, what do you watch?" He seemed to be asking Teri.

"Well, Speed TV and ESPN Racing," Teri replied.

"What do you read?" she felt to be the next question God was asking. Her reply? "Books about racing."

Then, "When you pray, what do you pray for?" Teri: "Wouldn't I look good in a Coca-Cola-sponsored outfit? Lord, I need a win in racing."

She felt that God was then asking, "Teri, what's number one?"

And she realized that racing had become her god—her top priority.

She prayed, "Lord, I've taken you off the throne. I've made racing the king. I want to put you back on the throne."

Shouldn't we ask ourselves those questions? Shouldn't we seek to discover what in our life is taking the place of God? When we find out, we must set it aside, for we must realize that at all times—from the best of times to the worst—how vital it is that we lean on God.

The Bible Addresses Leaning on God

"Let all who take refuge in you be glad." (Psalm 5:11)

"Commit your way to the Lord; trust in him and he will do this: He will make your righteousness shine like the dawn, the justice of your cause like the noonday sun." (Psalm 37:5–6)

"Is any one of you in trouble? He should pray." (James 5:13)

"The prayer of a righteous man is powerful and effective." (James 5:16)

Chad Hennings

Stick to It

*No one who puts his hand to the plow and looks back is fit
for service in the kingdom of God.*
—Luke 9:62

REMEMBER THOSE TIMES WHEN YOU SAT AT
the piano and wished you could be anywhere else in the world but there?
You'd rather be shoveling out horse barns than sitting at the keyboard
plunking out "She'll be Comin' Around the Mountain" for the eighteenth
time?

Or that time when you thought it would be a really good idea to run
cross country in high school, but by the second mile of your first race you
were already in one hundred twenty-third place and every organ in your
body was telling you to stop the madness?

Remember why you kept going in those or similar circumstances?

Mom. Or Dad. Or Coach. Or your teacher. All telling you, "You can't
quit." "Quitters never win." "If you quit now, you'll quit at everything."

For the most part, they were right. Commitment is vital to success in
life. And if ever there was a poster person for commitment, it is Chad Hennings.

See, Chad heard those warnings from his parents, and he heeded them.
When he wanted to quit, they wouldn't let him. And you know he had to
have strong parents to face down a guy who eventually would become a six-
foot-six-inch defensive lineman who played in three Super Bowls for the
Dallas Cowboys.

Of course, when Chad was a kid, albeit a large one, his folks had no
idea that when they taught him about commitment it would lead to the
remarkable circumstances he would enjoy as an adult. All they knew was
that if Chad began something, he was going to finish it.

And therein lies the secret to a ten-year stretch of time that most young
boys can only dream about.

But let's start when Hennings was a kid, growing up on a farm in Iowa.

One of his earliest memories of taking a job and sticking to it even
when it became drudgery was when he and his brother Todd decided to

have a 4-H project—grooming steers for competition. To do that, the boys had to feed them twice a day, halter-train them, groom them, make sure their hair was cut and combed, and train them to walk properly in preparation for the showings at fairs. When a kid is twelve or thirteen, that's a huge undertaking. Both Todd and Chad were successful too. One of their steers became a Grand Champion and the other a finalist for the award.

Chad also learned about commitment when he tried his hand at music. When he was young, he told his mom that he wanted to play the guitar. So his parents got him a guitar and they started him on guitar lessons. True to form for a youngster, it took about three weeks for him to get tired of those tedious lessons and all that plucking and picking. He wanted to quit.

But his mom hauled out the family motto, which was, "Once you start something, you never quit." So year after year Chad took lessons. Three years into it, he was ready to run over the guitar with the tractor. But he couldn't quit. Wasn't allowed to. For six years in all, he kept at it. Still today, Hennings says he appreciates that his mom made him keep at it.

The same thing happened a little later with drums and the school band. Playing the drums looked like a cool thing to do at the beginning of September. But before October rolled around, young Chad realized that he was no Ringo Starr. Didn't matter. He started the year on the drums, and he finished the school year the following May, still banging away.

When Hennings was in high school, he faced a crisis of commitment that would teach valuable lessons. As a freshman, he had been a member of the wrestling team, and he had proved to be a good grappler. But as his sophomore season rolled around, he had some fears about getting back on the mat. He feared the intensity of the one-on-one competition and the nervousness that went with each match. He also dreaded the possibility of having to cut weight to get into the proper weight class. He talked to his dad about it, and they decided that not wrestling as a sophomore was not quitting because he had not gone out for the team. Instead, Chad played basketball that winter.

But after the season, he began to think again about wrestling and about the fact that he wanted to prove to himself that he was not afraid of the man-to-man combat it offered. He returned to wrestling his junior year and excelled. As a senior, he was the state heavyweight wrestling champ.

In a sense, Hennings slipped a little on the commitment chart by opting out of wrestling as a sophomore, but he says it taught him "that you can never be successful if you fail to face your fears. Running from my fears would never make them go away. Only when I faced my fears could I conquer them." So, in effect, when he did kind of quit at something, he discovered the error of such a course.

Which brings us to another time of true commitment that Chad Hennings was forced to face.

Besides being a great wrestler, Hennings was an outstanding football player in high school. He took that ability with him when he went to the Air Force Academy in Colorado Springs, Colorado, for his university training. While at the Air Force, he excelled under legendary coach Fisher De-Berry.

After his second year at the Academy, he and all other second-year students were given the option of leaving the Academy. If, however, they signed up to stay, they were also committing themselves to stay with the Air Force for a number of years after graduation. Hennings wanted to be a pilot, and to do that, he would have to stay. He would have to make a commitment that would, in all likelihood, eliminate his chances of playing professional football. He had the skills and the size and the mentality—but if he signed up, he wouldn't have the freedom.

He signed. Hello cockpit, good-bye NFL.

Sure enough, at the end of his four years playing for the Air Force, the NFL was interested. And it wasn't just any team. It was the Dallas Cowboys. America's team. And you don't get more American than Chad Hennings.

The Cowboys were interested enough in this guy who couldn't possibly play for them that they used an eleventh-round draft pick to get him. He signed a small bonus that committed him to the Cowboys.

But first there was that other commitment. Funny how commitments can get in the way of each other. The Cowboys would have to wait. The U.S. government would not.

So Chad Hennings fulfilled his commitment to the Air Force. He learned to fly the A–10 Thunderbolt—otherwise known as the Warthog. He even flew his Warthog on missions into Iraq after the first Gulf War in the early 1990s.

In 1992, to his benefit, the U.S. military did some downsizing, and he was released from the last two years of his military obligation. This enabled him to join the Dallas Cowboys, where his commitment to keeping himself in top shape paid off in a fine NFL career and those three Super Bowl rings.

Commitment taught by his parents and continued through his own faith and dedication to doing his best for God at all times indeed paid off for Chad Hennings.

Looking Up

How about another farm story?

As this story goes, a young man named Jacob was enraptured by a beautiful girl named Rachel. When Jake asked Rachel's dad for her hand, he demanded a huge commitment: Give me seven years of work, and you can marry Rachel.

So Jake fulfilled his obligation. He labored the agreed-on seven years, and then there was a wedding. When Jacob awoke the morning after, he discovered that his new father-in-law, Laban, had tricked him into marrying Rachel's older sister.

Jacob was told that to win Rachel's hand, he would have to go back to work for seven more years. This time Laban came through, and Jacob married Rachel. But Jacob wasn't done. He gave Laban seven more years of work.

When we really want to achieve something, commitment comes easier. In our lives as Christians, what is our goal? If it is to bring glory to God through our lives, then we must face that task with a commitment that mirrors Jacob's commitment to Laban.

Our most important task as believers is to glorify God in everything we do. That takes commitment, because it is easy sometimes to forget who we are doing things for.

Another vital task God asks us to do is to love our neighbors as ourselves. This is where commitment really gets tested. Dealing with people can lead to frustrations that make us want to avoid those who cause us trouble. But if we are truly dedicated to serving others as a way of honoring God, we stay committed to showing Christlike love and Spirit-led compassion.

The Bible Addresses Commitment

"God tested Abraham. He said to him, 'Abraham!' 'Here I am,' he replied. Then God said, 'Take your son, your only son, Isaac, whom you love, and go to the region of Moriah. Sacrifice him there as a burnt offering on one of the mountains I will tell you about.' Early the next morning Abraham got up and saddled his donkey. He took with him two of his servants and his son Isaac." (Genesis 22:1–3)

"Praise awaits you, O God, in Zion; to you our vows will be fulfilled." (Psalm 65:1)

"Then a teacher of the law came to him and said, 'Teacher, I will follow you wherever you go.' Jesus replied, 'Foxes have holes and birds of the air have nests, but the Son of Man has no place to lay His head.' Another disciple said to him, 'Lord, first let me go and bury my father.' But Jesus told him, 'Follow me, and let the dead bury their own dead.'" (Matthew 8:19–22)

"Therefore, I urge you, brothers, in view of God's mercy, to offer your bodies as living sacrifices, holy and pleasing to God—this is your spiritual act of worship." (Romans 12:1)

Jon Kitna

Taking One for the Team

We put up with anything rather than hinder the gospel of Christ.
—1 Corinthians 9:13

IN THE WORLD OF PROFESSIONAL FOOTBALL,
there are several ways teams can say thank-you to their quarterbacks for a
job well done.

They can give him a fat raise and extend his contract into the next
decade.

They can have the public relations staff hype the player and make sure
he gets good publicity.

They can name a street near the stadium for him.

Or they can move him down the depth chart, hand him a cap and a
clipboard, and let him stand along the sidelines for a season or two.

Tom Brady. Peyton Manning. Donovan McNabb. They all got choices
one and two. John Elway got the first three.

Jon Kitna got what was behind door number four.

In 2003, Jon Kitna took a professional football team with a history of
failure and embarrassment and guided it to a respectable 8–8 record. He did
yeoman's work as he stood behind center for every single offensive snap of
the sixteen-game season. He passed for 3,591 yards and 15 touchdowns.

The team was the Cincinnati Bengals—at the time a woebegone fran-
chise that had eked out two wins the previous season. But a new skipper
was at the helm—Marvin Lewis—and a new attitude was brewing next to
the Ohio River in the Queen City.

When Kitna guided the Bengals to that .500 season, it wasn't the first
time he had surprised football experts with his prowess. After all, his high
school career was so ignored by college coaches that he wasn't even offered a
scholarship to the school of his choice: Washington State University. Oh,
the University of Washington did call. But they got in touch with Jon to ask
him about one of his high school teammates. A kid named Lawyer Milloy
(who turned out to be a pretty good college player and has had a successful
pro career at safety).

So with little interest from the big boys, Kitna went to an NAIA school,

Central Washington. And even then it wasn't because anybody there really wanted him to play football.

The quarterback coach didn't even know his name.

It seems that the only people who were interested in recruiting Jon Kitna were the gangs that circulated in the not-so-nice part of Tacoma, Washington, where he grew up. Toughened by that atmosphere and able to escape the mean streets, Kitna went ahead with his desire to play college football.

He stuck around at Central Washington, and by the time he was a senior, he was leading the Wildcats to the NAIA national championship.

But before that could happen, Kitna had to overcome a huge problem. Himself. He had conquered the football challenge, but by the time he was a sophomore and the starting QB, he had become what far too many away-from-home-kids become at college: a drunk.

Well, and a thief. And just for good measure, he cheated on his girlfriend.

He was barely twenty years old, and he was self-destructing his life as fast as he was building his football career.

But then he turned to a friend, Eric Boles, a wide receiver for the New York Jets. Boles and Kitna talked by phone, and the NFL guy told the college guy how to put his faith in Jesus Christ—how to have his burden of all those sins wiped away.

A few weeks later, while watching an NFL game, Kitna took a knee and trusted Jesus Christ as his Savior.

Suddenly everything changed, and Jon Kitna became a model citizen.

Okay, not everything changed. He still didn't get the right people's attention on the football field. Therefore, when the NFL drafted its players in the spring of 1996, Jon Kitna's name was not called.

Undeterred, Kitna signed as an undrafted free agent with the Seattle Seahawks and, just as he did in college, set out to prove everybody wrong. This time, though, he took God with him. And that change in his life would be the thing that would cause so many people to sit up and take notice of the classy, yes, godly way Kitna would handle what seemed to be a huge snub by the Cincinnati coaching staff in 2004.

The selflessness Kitna showed in 2004, though, didn't come without some practice. He got plenty of it in Seattle, where it seemed that no matter what he did, the Seahawks had a reason to replace him.

Take the 2000 season. In 1999, Kitna led the Seahawks to the playoffs, starting fifteen games and helping the team to a 9–7 record. So in 2000, just five games into the season, he was back on the sidelines as Damon Huard was given the ball. By 2001, Kitna was off to Cincinnati via free agency.

And then came the success of 2003, followed by the snub of 2004.

The Bengals relegated Kitna to the sidelines. Let's say you're in Cincinnati at the time, reading the newspapers. You can see the headlines: "Kitna Protests Snub," "QB Requests Trade," "Bengal Signal-Caller Lashes Out."

Never happened. Those were not the headlines that would describe the way Jon Kitna accepted stepping aside for second-year quarterback Carson Palmer.

Or try imagining this. You look down on the field and you see Kitna stare down Palmer on the sidelines—refusing to talk to him. What if the kid were to ask for advice? At your own risk, C. P.

Again, those things never happened.

Instead, Kitna became Carson Palmer's biggest booster.

How did he do it? How did a guy who has worked so stinking hard to get to the top of his profession handle things with such class? Because he thinks right.

"I think the thing that helped me the most in terms of getting over the disappointment of losing my job was Jeremiah 29:11–13," says Kitna. "Those verses clearly state that God has a plan for my life, and since I know that God is in total control of all things—and yes, even seemingly trivial things as an NFL depth chart—for me to complain and cause a fuss would really be an indictment of my faith in the living God."

We're talking about a gritty performer here. A get-your-uniform-dirty kind of quarterback. A get-the-job-done signal-caller. But Kitna understands that joy in life is found not in your circumstances but in how you handle them. "The joy that has come as a result of this circumstance in my life is first, a great peace and confidence in knowing I am in the will of God. Second, I have been able to encourage so many people who in the world's eyes have been dealt a bad hand. Third, is the incredible friendship that I have gained with Carson as a result. He is truly my best friend on the team."

When the Cincinnati Bengals clinched a playoff spot during the 2005 season, guess who grabbed the handles of the Gatorade to dump it all over the wise head of coach Marvin Lewis? Carson Palmer had one side of the tub and Jon Kitna had the other. Their partnership, both in football and in faith, shows what selflessness is all about. Palmer waited patiently and uncomplainingly through his first NFL season as Kitna became the first Bengal in team history to throw every pass in a season. And then Kitna stepped aside selflessly when Lewis determined that Palmer was ready to take over.

"I have always believed that God had Carson and me in Cincinnati at the same time so I can be an example of what it means to be a godly man who happens to play quarterback in the NFL. I hope this time has been as big a blessing to him as it was to me."

After the 2005 season, Kitna moved on to Detroit, once more to show his importance as a teammate and a quarterback.

Who could ever ask for a better teammate than Jon Kitna?

Looking Up

Free? When we trust Jesus Christ as Savior, aren't we set free? And in being set free, shouldn't we be allowed to say anything or do anything when we are slighted?

Isn't that the way freedom works?

The apostle Paul thought about that question, and with the help of the Holy Spirit telling him the right answer, said, "Though I am free and belong to no man, I make myself a slave to everyone" (1 Corinthians 9:19).

Our freedom in Christ is not a freedom from relationships. It is a freedom to love as Jesus loves and to give as Jesus gives.

Sometimes we mistake freedom for anarchy—that if we are truly free, there is nothing or no one who has any say over what we do. We do what we please when we please.

We think Jon Kitna ought to stand up for himself and lash out at the unfairness of it all.

Wrong. Freedom in Christ means that we are free from the shackles of sin and degradation, but we are at the same time subject to others. We have a responsibility as free people in Christ to care for others, be kind to others, treat others the way we want to be treated.

Freedom in Christ does not give us the right to mistreat others or hold grudges against them. Freedom in Christ is so powerful that it allows us to love when others hate, care when others don't, give when others take, forgive when others can't.

It is not circumstances that should control how we treat others. It is Jesus. We are Jesus to others when we surround them with unconditional love and undeniable compassion. We are Jesus to others when we take a slight and let it slip away without retaliation.

"I make myself a slave to everyone," Paul said.

How can we do that today in a way that will bring glory to God?

The Bible Addresses Selflessness

"Though I am free and belong to no man, I make myself a slave to everyone." (1 Corinthians 9:19)

"Love . . . is not self-seeking." (1 Corinthians 13:4–5)

"Nobody should seek his own good, but the good of others." (1 Corinthians 10:24)

"Do nothing out of selfish ambition or vain conceit, but in humility consider others better than yourselves. Each of you should look not only to your own interests, but also to the interests of others." (Philippians 2:3–4)

"Love your neighbor as yourself." (James 2:8)

25

Jeremy VanSchoonhoven
Standing Strong

But Daniel resolved not to defile himself.
—Daniel 1:8

WHAT JEREMY VANSCHOONHOVEN DOES while riding a bicycle could best be described as unusual.

And that begins with the name of what he does. It's called Observed Bike Trials. If that does not conjure up images of guys flying off ramps doing backflips or some other dangerous trick, well, that's okay.

Observed Bike Trials are not about flying through the air toward a questionable future. They are not about making a BMX bicycle do things that should make it come apart in midair. In fact, VanSchoonhoven himself has observed, "The worst thing I've ever done is hit my shin and split it open."

But that doesn't mean it's as safe as walking the dog.

The men and women who compete in Observed Bike Trials do not major in high-flying, faster-than-safe, look-out-below tricks. Instead, they concentrate—and concentrate hard—on precision. The action can be slow, and it always takes mental preparation, patience, strength, and extreme care.

Here's an example of the kinds of things that an Observed Bike Trials expert does: Pallet climbing.

Do not try this at home.

A bunch of pallets are stacked up fifty-four or so inches high. The rider's job is to get on top of the pallets without a ramp (or a crane). To do this (as VanSchoonhoven describes it), he rides at high speed toward the stack and smacks his front tire against the wooden obstacle. The bike's momentum somehow (you'd need a physics teacher to take it from here) bounces the bike and the rider upward, and he inexplicably pulls a major wheelie that enables him to pull himself to the top of the pallets.

According to VanSchoonhoven, it took him about two years to learn how to do this. He didn't say how many bikes, pallets, or teeth he went through in the process.

Other maneuvers an Observed Bike Trials rider would endeavor to accomplish include riding wheelies across moss-covered creek beds, crossing huge boulders, and negotiating hairpin curves on steep downhill descents of uncharted mountains.

To get through all of this and to compete with some of the top Observed Bike Trials riders in the world with a torn-up shin is pretty good. But something else Jeremy negotiated was just as impressive spiritually.

See, Jeremy grew up in a relatively sheltered environment in the Great Northwest. Williams, Oregon, was home, and his family lived on a farm. His basic influences were his family and his farm. And, of course, his faith. Jeremy trusted Jesus Christ as his Savior as a kid through his parents' influence, and when he was seventeen, he "got on fire for God." He decided that he should "get out of there and live my life for God and share Him with others."

That's a great idea and all, but it's a lot easier to say that from the kitchen of a farmhouse in Oregon than it is from the situations in which Jeremy would soon find himself.

Jeremy had been riding since he was twelve, gradually moving up the ladder of Observed Bike Trials success. He had placed sixth in a World Cup Race at age fifteen. Over the next few years, he had made such a name for himself that the logical next step was to go pro—to leave home and compete on the professional circuit with sponsors and everything.

That, of course, would mean working with and competing against men and women who did not always share Jeremy's love for Jesus Christ. That is something everyone who names the name of Christ must face, but with professional athletes, the possibility of being overwhelmed by a differing lifestyle seems to take on greater magnitude.

Especially for a youngster.

"I was one of the youngest pros ever in the United States," VanSchoonhoven says. "All those guys that I look up to are now asking me to go out drinking with them and partying with them."

That, for the ungrounded, undedicated Christian, can be trouble. Mom's not there to remind you of all those great verses about avoiding temptation. Dad's not there to remind you about little things like losing your inheritance. Little brother's not there as a reminder of your testimony.

But VanSchoonhoven's full-fledged faith and his strong commitment made it possible for him to shine in the darkness.

"It was really tough," Jeremy says in an understatement.

And it wasn't just the partying he was willing to give up.

"I lost a lot of things because I said no." VanSchoonhoven recalls. "A bunch of the guys had really good connections with sponsors and stuff. If I had just hung out with them, they would have hooked me up so I could've gotten a free car and thirty thousand bucks a year and all this different stuff. It was a big trade-off."

Bad move, right? Wasting all those good vibes over a little thing like morality? After all, in this day of everything goes, who's going to know the difference anyway? Why not just live a little and ask for forgiveness later? Looking back now, surely he's a bit sorry he went to all that follow-the-rules goodness, don't you think?

Not a chance.

"I'm definitely glad I made the decision I did."

There's something to that sowing and reaping idea. Jeremy sowed boldness and he reaped benefits.

Now Jeremy VanSchoonhoven is the veteran. Now he's the guy the younger riders look up to—and they respect him for his stance.

"Everybody knows that I'm a Christian. They don't really mind. Some of them make comments behind my back, but some of them I've had really good talks with. I get to talk to people about Christ—people who hardly anybody would get a chance to talk to. And it's just because they respect me for my bike riding."

The first word of Jeremy's sport is *observed,* which is also a good description of the life he lives as a Christian among the others who dangle their bikes off boulders and balance them on I-beams. No, it's not normal to take a *bike* places he does, but as he does it, he also displays what might be seen as an abnormal ability to show off his faith at the same time. And if he has a few *trials* along the way, he's ready for the fallout.

Observed Bike Trials. Nothing fits better for what Jeremy Van-Schoonhoven does than that.

Looking Up

When Jeremy decided to sell out to God, he was about the same age as a transplanted teenager from Israel whose life was also under extreme observation. Daniel and his buddies had been selected as kind of an All-Star team of teens headed for success. They were called into the king's court and told that they would be required to partake of a sumptuous diet that would guarantee their good health and success in the court.

But just as Jeremy boldly said no to the easy way to success and fortune, they courageously said no to the easy ladder of success in the kingdom of Babylon. They knew that the food and drink being offered to them would violate the restrictions that they as Jews were to live under, so they turned down the menu.

The people who were in charge decided to give them a chance—to observe them as they ate a different diet. Daniel and his friends passed the trial, and they impressed the judges with their countenance.

Translated into twenty-first-century language, this story could go like this.

A Christian kid makes it to his senior year of high school without having sampled drugs and alcohol. But in his senior year, he begins to get the business from his friends. "What kind of wimp are you? Won't even take a drink! Afraid of what Mommy will say?"

What the kid does next depends on whether he has, as Daniel did, "purposed in his heart" to do the right thing. If he has made a vow to avoid entanglements that might bring him down, he will have already decided on the answer before the question comes up.

Daniel had already made his decision before it was time to make a decision.

So had Jeremy.

Have you? Have you told God that you will avoid giving in to things that you know are either clearly sinful or are not expedient or are not going to enhance your testimony for Jesus?

Whether you're a teenager in the king's court, a young man riding bikes with the champions, or a B-average student on the debate team—the decision will tell a lot about your true allegiance.

The Bible Addresses Standing Strong

"And now, dear children, continue in him, so that when he appears we may be confident and unashamed before him at his coming." (1 John 2:28)

"Now, Lord, consider their threats and enable your servants to speak your word with great boldness." (Acts 4:29)

"So Paul and Barnabas spent considerable time there, speaking boldly for the Lord, who confirmed the message of his grace by enabling them to do miraculous signs and wonders." (Acts 14:3)

Betsy King
Caring Till It Helps

I tell you the truth, whatever you did for
one of the least of these brothers of mine, you did for me.
—Matthew 25:40

YOU CAN MAKE SOME ASSUMPTIONS about
Betsy King. For one thing, because she has made $7 million or so as a Hall
of Fame golfer on the LPGA Tour, you can assume right away that she has
had the freedom to travel. Wealthy people usually take trips.

Cancun. Paris. Bermuda. All the hot spots that people who don't have to
score big savings on Priceline.com go to.

And you might assume that because she made a career of hanging
around country clubs (and you know that's where the really rich people are),
she's a hobnobber who wants nothing to do with the little people.

Well, if you were to make those assumptions based on the simple fact
that Betsy King had a long, successful, lucrative career as a golfer, you'd be
so wrong you should turn in your LPGA media guide.

No matter what happened to Betsy King as a professional golfer, it did
not turn her into a prima donna who is too big for her golf pants. In fact,
playing professional golf all those years and with all that success, she feels,
was just a preliminary to greater things she could do for others.

What Betsy was able to do with others went beyond the normal visit-
kids-in-the-hospital-for-a-couple-of-hours kind of thing, as important as
those visits are from pro athletes. And what she did also forced her to get
outside of what she calls the "self-centered" world of professional golf, where
the athletes have to, because of the nature of individual sports, always worry
about "taking care of yourself, always for the goal of playing golf well," as
she puts it.

In effect, King says, her efforts went along with her goal of "intention-
ally using golf to help others."

It all began for Betsy when she was introduced to the ministry Habitat
for Humanity. That led her to become involved, with other golfers, in
building homes for people in need. She and others have worked to build
homes in both Phoenix, Arizona, and Charlotte, North Carolina.

But what has really touched a hot button with Betsy in her quest to use what God has given her to help others is her work in lands outside the United States.

One such trip took her to Korea. Working with Links Players International, she traveled there to use golf as a ministry by playing and teaching the game, similar to what traveling basketball and soccer teams do. She played the game with groups of Koreans, and she was able to share her faith in Jesus Christ with them.

While there, she began to grow in her appreciation for people who lived far differently from how we live in North America. For instance, while in Korea, she noticed that the folks who owned the golf courses had strung cables across the fairways. She learned that it was so if North Korea were to invade South Korea, they couldn't land airplanes on the golf course. That opened her eyes to people who live with different realities and worries than who's going to win the next golf tournament.

Betsy's travels continued as she sought more ways to help others. One of her best friends and spiritual leaders, Cris Stevens, who has been the Bible study leader on the LPGA Tour for a long time, helped set up a visit to Romania for Betsy and other LPGA players. It was shortly after the reign of Romanian leader Nicolae Ceausescu had ended, and the country was slowly coming out from under the oppression of communism.

In the news at the time were the deplorable conditions of some orphanages in Romania. A family Stevens knew went to Romania to help, and they helped set up an initial visit in 1993.

"We visited several orphanages," King explains. "One reason we went was to support the missionaries. We played with the kids a lot."

It was an eye-opener for the ladies as they saw so many kids in need.

In 1994, King and others returned, a single fact that she knows meant a lot to the people they visited again. "So many people say, 'We'll be back,' but they don't return," she says.

This time, in addition to visiting the orphanages, they were asked to crawl out of their comfort zone and become a singing group. "One of the golfers knew how to play the guitar," King says, "so we just followed her. We had to get up on stage in a church and sing."

It must have gone pretty well, for they also sang door-to-door and even sang once in a train station.

During that exhibition, she was reminded of how different things were in Romania when one of the Romanians with them remarked, "You would have been arrested for doing that just a couple of years ago."

King thinks back to that situation and says, "I wonder how I would have responded if I would have had to live like that."

It's not just Korea and Romania that has King's heart. In 2001, she helped support the Drive for Life, an effort to help people in Tanzania. Through that golf-related fund-raiser, $225,000 was raised. When the tragedy of 9/11 struck, the plans of King, Stevens, and others to deliver the money firsthand in Tanzania were thwarted. But the money was still distributed to the needy there.

More recently, King has been involved in various ventures for World Vision. One example was a visit in 2005 to Honduras. She traveled there with 2003 women's U.S. Open champion Hilary Lunke and her husband, Tyler. While there, they saw firsthand a project that is saving lives. World Vision, recognizing a danger in home construction in Honduras, is trying to make a difference.

Many of the people live in thatched-roof homes, but in that thatch often live bugs that transmit a deadly illness called Chagas. In addition, the homes often have poorly ventilated woodstoves, which lead to respiratory illnesses in children. So King and the Lunkes were there to help—and to play with the kids, many of whom were supported by World Vision donations.

Why in the world does Betsy King travel so much to help others? "This is the way God made me," she says. "God has put it in my heart to help, as Jesus said, 'the least of these.' I realized I can't change the whole world, but I've been told that we still should 'change the world we're in.' One of the things that kept me in golf was the opportunity it gave me to help others and to get others to help."

So yes, Betsy King made a bundle of money, and she is able to travel. But wouldn't it be great if we had more pro athletes who used their money and their freedom for such a grand cause as encouraging and lifting up those with so little?

Looking Up

How often have you read about Christian athletes in secular publications and been disappointed when instead of saying something like, "Jane Athlete trusts Jesus as her Savior and lives to serve Him," the article says, "Jane Athlete is religious." Most of the time, that doesn't clearly describe athletes who are living for the Savior. Most of the time, it's a non-Christian's confused way of trying to describe something he or she does not understand.

However, if a writer were to describe Betsy King as "religious," that would be right on target. According to God's Word, true religion is not practicing a set of beliefs or going to church or not chewing tobacco. "Religion that our Father accepts as pure and faultless is this: To visit orphans and widows . . ." (1:27). That's what James, the brother of Jesus, says, and since it's in God's holy Word, it's undoubtedly a great way to describe our task on earth.

So what do we do with Betsy's example now that we've seen it in action? How do we incorporate in our lives this care for those with less?

First, we review what Jesus said when He explained that if we do good deeds for those in need, we are doing good deeds for our Savior himself. That will help us be loving and help others truly altruistically and without pride, for how humbling is it to do something that Jesus would see as something done for Him?

Second, we must see how God has equipped us. Some are gifted in math and science—and they can tutor younger kids. Others can sing in the choir and perform on the drumline—providing entertainment for others. Some like to plan school functions or church mission trips. Each person has a different gift and a different set of interests. But we can all do something in the name of Jesus.

What better way can we reflect our heavenly Father's love and honor His free gift of salvation to us than by reaching out and giving to others?

The Bible Addresses Helping

"Blessed is he who has regard for the weak; the Lord delivers him in times of trouble." (Psalm 41:1)

"He who is kind to the poor lends to the Lord, and he will reward him for what he has done." (Proverbs 19:17)

"Share your food with the hungry and . . . provide the poor wanderer with shelter." (Isaiah 58:7)

David Pollack
Discernment

Be very careful, then, how you live—not as unwise but as wise,
making the most of every opportunity, because the days are evil.
—*Ephesians 5:15–16*

THIS IS ABOUT DAVID POLLACK, NFL LINE-
backer. But it's not just about him. It's about David and a bunch of other brave young men who stood up to a growing culture of sensuality and lack of concern for purity.

This is about making a tough decision that can lead to derision, embarrassment, and mockery. This is about letting an ancient, timeless book intervene in deciding not to be involved with a more recent publication that stands opposed to that ancient book in so many ways.

It's about guys: NFL players like André Davis and Rocky Calmus.

David Pollack played college football at the University of Georgia. While a Bulldog, he played for one of the finest Christian coaches in the land, Mark Richt. It made for a grand combination of two men of faith who could lift each other up and spur each other on to spiritual strength.

Among the challenges Pollack faced as a Christian in the world of major college football happened in the spring of 2003. As a talented lineman with clear NFL-draft credentials, Pollack attracted the attention of many publications who named All-American teams. Most of those publications simply called the school, got a headshot of Pollack, and then he showed up in their pages as a preseason All-American.

One publication, though, wanted to do much more for Pollack and his fellow All-Americans. This publication wanted to fly him to California, provide him with posh accommodations, show him some good times, and, of course, take his picture for inclusion in its preseason All-American college football preview.

Cool, huh?

Maybe not. This publication is one that has been attempting to change the morals of Americans for the past fifty years. It is one that features provocative photos of unclothed females—and articles that promote a lifestyle of godless hedonism. This publication is *Playboy*.

Yes, it is the twenty-first century, and perhaps the days when everyone considered *Playboy* pornographic were left behind with the passing of Y2K, but that doesn't mean its pages violate Scripture any less than they did in 1955. The Bible still clearly stands diametrically opposed to the sexual revolution touted by *Playboy*. Association with this publication continues to represent connections with ungodliness and immorality.

And David Pollack, while living in a college community among who knows how many free-thinking, anything-goes fellow students, stood his ground. He said no to *Playboy* and its request for him to be one of its All-Americans.

That is discernment.

And that is not easy.

"It was nice that they thought enough of me to select me for that honor," Pollack says of the magazine's attempt to put him on their All-American team. "But to me, turning down that 'honor' was a no-brainer."

It was before Pollack's junior year at the University of Georgia. Pollack was so good that people were suggesting that he might win the Bronco Nagurski Trophy, which is given to the best defensive player in the land.

The folks at *Playboy* called the public relations people at Georgia and told them to ask David to set up a time when he could do the photo shoot. When the people at Georgia told David about it, he had a ready answer. He wasn't interested.

"I had been talking to churches and youth groups. I had told the kids about living right and doing right. I told them to be careful who they associated with. It wouldn't have been right to be associated with a magazine like *Playboy*."

Pollack, of course, got some grief for his decisions. Some of his teammates said, "What are you doing, turning that down?"

And he received a bit of criticism by the media.

Not that he heard any of that. "I learned after my sophomore year not to listen to or read what people say about me. I had a good year, and everybody started saying how good I was. I had to stop listening to it."

But his mom heard some of the criticsm, and she told him about it.

"I still didn't care what they said. Isaiah 43:7 says I was created for God's glory. Not my glory."

The bottom line for David Pollack? "That publication is not honoring to Christ, and I didn't want to be a part of it."

Rocky Calmus is another guy who decided to stay home rather than put himself into a compromising situation with the magazine. He too suggests that making such a choice was not as hard as it may sound.

"It wasn't really a tough decision I had to think about—because of the way I was brought up and how my faith was growing at the time."

Calmus, who attended the University of Oklahoma and started his NFL career in 2002, says that "through high school and college, I was growing in my faith and in my walk with God. It was just something I didn't want to be associated with or support." He was speaking of the request *Playboy* made for him to be involved while he was at Oklahoma.

"I felt like I would be a hypocrite [because of] the things I stand for, to then go ahead and receive an award from there," Calmus went on to say.

When Calmus made his decision, as often happens with these kinds of things, the story made the news, which shows something about the culture we live in. Take a strong moral stand; make the headlines.

When it did hit the papers, Calmus' story affected others, including Wesley Britt, who was playing football for the University of Alabama. He read about Calmus' stand, and he remembered it. Then two years later, after he had carved out an All-American career for the Crimson Tide, he too got a call from the purveyor of porn.

"Calmus showed that it was okay that people do decline it," Britt later declared. "He kind of paved the road for others to make that decision—that it was all right. It made it a little easier to decline a great honor. Seeing Rocky's faith made my faith that much stronger."

Another athlete who took a cue from previous brave football players regarding this decision was André Davis, who played for Virginia Tech before moving on to the NFL in 2002. Before he began his college years at Blacksburg, he noticed how Danny Wuerffel handled this situation. He also got wise advice from his future wife, Janelle, and from his parents, who all told him that if he were to refuse the award, God would send him special blessings.

"I think through God's blessing and His will, He allowed my college graduation to be on the same day [as his scheduled photo shoot]. I knew I was going to be at my graduation rather than going and taking a picture."

For André Davis, the reason behind his refusal went beyond a problem in scheduling, though. "I may ruin somebody else's relationship with Christ because they feel like that would be okay [if I was in the magazine]."

Wise living by some careful Christians—standing up and standing out for what they believe.

Looking Up

The Bible is silent on a lot of subjects that we wish it spoke about clearly.

You can put together a long list of subjects that are controversial for Christians but that are not addressed in the pages of holy writ.

Social dancing. Smoking cigarettes. Going to movies. Playing the lottery. Playing sports on Sunday. Add your own questionable activities.

Instead, what the Bible gives us are principles—guidelines that can help us make clear-headed decisions about questionable activities.

Look, for instance, at what Paul says in 1 Thessalonians 4 (3-4): "It is God's will that you be sanctified: that you should avoid sexual immorality; that each of you should learn to control his own body in a way that is holy and honorable."

It doesn't take a degree from Dallas Theological Seminary to figure out what God is saying through Paul. The principle is as clear: God wants you to live in a way that is "set apart," or "sanctified." And part of that is to be sexually pure.

Now, we could sit and debate specifically what that means, but perhaps something NFL superstar Shaun Alexander and his girlfriend decided will spell it out best. When Shaun and Valerie met, they immediately knew they were right for each other. But they weren't in any way ready to exchange rings and pick out curtains. So they decided this: If they never kissed each other before they got married, they would never sin sexually. So, they drew the line. The first time they kissed was when the pastor said to Shaun, "You may kiss your bride."

Sound extreme? Maybe a little. But it sure set them apart. It sure helped them avoid sexual immorality. And you can be sure it pleased God.

We can dance around God's standards and not take them seriously, but all that will do is cause us trouble—spiritually and physically.

Or we can use God's guidelines as a reminder to glorify Him, not ourselves.

That's wise living.

The Bible Addresses Discernment

"So give your servant a discerning heart to govern your people and to distinguish between right and wrong." (1 Kings 3:9)

"I am your servant; give me discernment that I may understand your statutes." (Psalm 119:125)

"Now the Bereans were of more noble character than the Thessalonians, for they received the message with great eagerness and examined the Scriptures every day to see if what Paul said was true." (Acts 17:11)

"The man without the Spirit does not accept the things that come from the Spirit of God, for they are foolishness to him, and he cannot understand them, because they are spiritually discerned. The spiritual man makes judgments about all things, but he himself is not subject to any man's judgment: 'For who has known the mind of the Lord that he may instruct Him?'" (1 Corinthians 2:14–16)

A. C. Green

Practicing Purity

*Flee from sexual immorality. All other sins a man commits are
outside his body, but he who sins sexually sins against his own body.*
—*1 Corinthians 6:18*

WHAT A. C. GREEN DID COULD MAKE NEWS only
because he lived in an age when morality was more of a surprise than
immorality. At one time in American culture, if one were to write about
A. C. Green's noteworthy accomplishment, most people would have read
about it and yawned. "So? What's the big deal with that?"

What was A. C. Green's accomplishment?

It was something he *didn't* do.

Green was a professional sports star in the 1980s and 1990s who
remained sexually pure throughout his entire career. What's even more outstanding is the fact that all the while he was standing up for sexual abstinence, Green was also setting a new standard for hard work and diligence.
During his NBA career, Green set the record for playing in the most consecutive games in league history.

You might say he was a man with two very admirable streaks, both
going on at the same time.

The consecutive game streak, which ended first, came when he retired
from the game in 2001 after suiting up and playing in 1,192 consecutive
games. The second streak—the one that made him the hero of many parents of teenagers—ended when A. C. Green got married in the spring of
2002 at the age of thirty-eight.

Two great streaks. One out of devotion to God and His teachings, and
the other . . . well, for the same reason.

The consecutive games streak, like the abstinence streak, didn't come
without obstacles. Along the way to 1,192 games, A. C. had to fight
through stuff that would have sidelined most players. In February 1995, he
lost two teeth to an opponent's elbow, but he played in the next game. For
the next twelve games, he wore a mask to protect what was left of his teeth.
He overcame food poisoning, stiff necks, torn thumb ligaments, and the
usual assortment of niggling injuries that come from running up and down

the court with other guys who are six foot nine and weigh 275 pounds—or more.

But it was his sexual abstinence that really captured everyone's attention.

When he was thirty-two years old, A. C. was asked by a reporter how he had maintained his virginity for so long. His reply could easily be applied to either his streak of avoiding sexual action or his streak of tough court action.

"I've stuck to it, but it's only been by God's grace," he replied. "I keep looking to Him to be my source and power. But at the same time, I keep looking to Him because I love Him, I want to please Him, and I want to be committed to Him. Those various ingredients on both sides of the scale are enough to keep anybody on the straight and narrow path."

Green turned the sexual abstinence streak into a campaign, using his A. C. Green Youth Foundation as a platform for attempting to influence young people to follow his example. He boldly proclaimed that his message was counterculture.

"The media, as well as professional athletes or entertainers or just people in general, state that the normal way, the natural way of sex is this: Have sex when you want to, but try to do it safe. We want to show the reasonableness of abstinence, which is waiting until you get married before you start having sex. Or stop having sex now, and wait out the period of time until you choose to get married."

He knew he was on to a good idea, and he never shied away from preaching his message of high quality morality. He knew, however, that not everyone agreed. "People admit that abstinence is good and that it is one of the best things, but they say that not many kids are going to do that or they've already had sex."

Green was even able to have a little fun with the fact that his lifestyle decision was not shared by most of the folks who populated the NBA. One thing Green did to promote his abstinence program was use a small green stuffed bear as the symbol of his campaign. The bear, called Little A. C., for Abstinence Committed, began appearing on the L.A. Lakers bench late in Green's career. At one game, A. C. had nineteen thousand of the bears handed out to the fans as they entered the arena for a Lakers game.

Reporters and cameramen couldn't get enough of Green's bear, often taking photos of him as he sat on the bench holding Little A. C. One time he put the bear on his head while sitting on the sidelines.

That prompted this scenario, which Green described in an *LA Times* article by Bill Plaschke. "I had a teammate come up to me and say, 'You don't know how silly you look with that bear on your head.' I told him, 'You don't know how silly you look when you're running around at night half drunk.'"

Those who covered the Lakers games and had to write about them for a living reacted variously to Green's use of the bear. Plaschke looked around at what was advertised in the arena and commented, "Compared to some products, perhaps we should not ridicule Green's message, but embrace it."

A more cynical approach was taken by Tim Keown, a writer for *ESPN The Magazine*. While writing an article on Green's little green pet, Keown declared, "Hard to imagine, but Green's action allows us to say that Phil Jackson did not coach his nuttiest power forward while with the Bulls." His reference, of course, was to the most bizarre human ever to play in the NBA, Dennis Rodman. Imagine someone even pretending to compare Green's clean, wholesome attempt to keep kids out of trouble to Rodman's outrageous antics.

A. C. Green was used to it, though.

From the beginning of his career as a youngster out of college, he faced a never-ending stream of teammates who couldn't imagine living with a standard so high. "You won't last two months in the NBA," he was told by some teammates when they learned the rookie was a virgin. They even tried to help him mend what they surely saw as the error of his ways. "Some even threatened to set me up with women they knew," he recalls about so-called friends who wanted to introduce him to women they thought he couldn't refuse. Sometimes they tried to trick him into compromising situations where women would be available.

He knew he was missing something good, but he was waiting for something much better. "Don't get me wrong. Sex itself isn't bad. It's just a matter of when to experience it. God created it for enjoyment, but He also reserved it for marriage. So, I'm waiting.

"Keeping my body pure from immorality is another part of my overall conditioning," he said in his book *Victory*. "It affects every part of my life, not just the physical. When I became a Christian, I made a vow like Samson's, but my strength wasn't in anything external; it was in my word. I resolved not to be with a woman until I married. My convictions were obvious when I joined the Lakers but not proven, so a few players taunted, teased, tempted, and tried me to see if I'd hold up to my standards."

A. C. was just too smart to be tricked out of what he knew to be right before God. He had already thought through his strategy.

"I always have a choice to make," Green says, thinking back on how he protected his purity. "If I'm tempted by some woman or even a TV commercial, I don't have to look. I exercise my power of choice to keep control of my own body, my own life. We all have the power of choice. But once used, our choice then has power over us. We have to live with the consequences."

Green took seriously his status as a role model to young people. "I want to be a man of integrity, one who is not just status quo about basketball—not the stereotypical athlete. My lifestyle, I believe, is totally different and contrary. I'm accountable for the talent and platform God has given me, and I want to use it to carry a message. A message that drives people to thinking and focusing on God and His goodness."

From Scripture he took his marching orders in that regard, leaning on the teaching of Psalm 71:17–18, which says, "Since my youth, O God, you have taught me, and to this day I declare your marvelous deeds. Even when I am old and gray, do not forsake me, O God, till I declare your power to the next generation, your might to all who are to come."

Scripture, determination, guts. Those are parts of the equation. But there is something else that marks a man of commitment—something A. C. revealed to sportswriter Rob Bentz in an interview for *Sports Spectrum* magazine. "My strength comes from the commitment that I have with God, because I have to have more than a vow. I have to have a relationship where He is my Savior. It starts by being committed to Jesus. That has been my anchor."

And to that add this: a three-pronged passion. Three things that fueled A. C. Green's fire to do what was right, no matter what anybody said or did about it. Passion one: "Fulfilling the purpose of God." Passion two: "To be a man of God. I want to believe God, to be constantly pursuing Him." Passion three: "Leading our future generation to their destiny."

"I want young people to hear this message: It is possible to wait. Not everybody is doing it."

A. C. Green waited, and for the rest of his life he and his wife will cherish their special relationship because one man was willing to trust that God knows what He is talking about.

Looking Up

If you say something enough times, think about it constantly, and believe it sincerely, does that make it true? Does that make it right?

In the beginning decade of the twenty-first century, our society is trying to say it over and over and over again: Sex outside of marriage does not matter.

Back in the 1960s, it was called the sexual revolution. One by one and then in huge numbers, people came along to proclaim that the backwoods idea that a young man and a young woman should not have sexual relations until they were married was as antiquated as the eight-track tape player. The modern age, they said, calls for throwing out the rules and letting everyone do whatever they feel like doing.

There's a problem with that.

You can't just throw out the rules and expect to avoid the penalty. Those standards are timeless, never-changing rules that God himself set forth in the pages of the book He wrote for us.

Scripture has laid out clear and unchangeable rules for sexual behavior, and to ignore them is to tell God that He is wrong. It is to make ourselves a little higher than the deity. It is to set ourselves up as authorities who know more than the One who created us.

Take a look at some of the standards:

"Marriage should be honored by all, and the marriage bed kept pure, for God will judge the adulterer and all the sexually immoral" (Hebrews 13:4).

"Flee from sexual immorality" (1 Corinthians 6:18).

"I have written you in my letter not to associate with sexually immoral people" (1 Corinthians 5:9).

The question of our sexual activity cannot be separated from our relationship with God.

If we, like Joseph of the Old Testament, run when sexual temptation stands in front of us (Genesis 39), we open ourselves to God's blessing. But if we cave in to it as King David did (2 Samuel 11), we set ourselves up for despair and disaster, as he did.

God cares deeply about whether we are pure in both heart and actions. The best way to honor our heavenly Father with our lives is to keep a vow of purity, to run from sexual temptation, and to live in a way that honors God's standards for us in regard to sexuality.

The Bible Addresses Purity

"But among you there must not be even a hint of sexual immorality, or of any kind of impurity." (Ephesians 5:3)

"The acts of the sinful nature are obvious: sexual immorality. . . ." (Galatians 5:19)

"Flee from sexual immorality. All other sins a man commits are outside his body, but he who sins sexually sins against his own body. Do you not know that your body is a temple of the Holy Spirit. . . ?" (1 Corinthians 6:18–19)

"Marriage should be honored by all, and the marriage bed kept pure, for God will judge the adulterer and all the sexually immoral." (Hebrews 13:4)

"Put to death, therefore, whatever belongs to your earthly nature: sexual immorality, impurity. . . ." (Colossians 3:5)

29

Erin Buescher
Ode to Joy

*Shout for joy to the Lord, all the earth. Worship the Lord
with gladness; come before him with joyful songs.*
—Psalm 100:1–2

WHEN WE FIRST PICK UP THE STORY, Erin Buescher
has, for some reason, lost it.

She has graduated from Rincon Valley Christian High School, where she
had it in abundance. Her talent on the basketball court and her popularity
among the students let it shine. She led her team to a state title, and she was
named Player of the Year in California.

Then it was off to the University of California at Santa Barbara, where
she could display it on a rather large canvas at a Division I university. There
she would parlay her size (she's six foot three), her shooting ability, and her
court sense into a successful college basketball career.

While playing for the Gauchos, she became an All-American. She was
on the fast track to the WNBA, it was clear. She spent three impressive
years making UCSB glad she was wearing number 11 for them.

But that's when she lost it.

Amid the accolades and the honors and the big-time victories, it went
away.

The joy, that is. Gone.

"I discovered that playing Division I hoops is similar to working a full-
time job" Buescher wrote in the *Sports Spectrum* magazine devotional book-
let, *Power Up!* "The joy I had once experienced through basketball was soon
gone. Worse than that, my relationship with the Lord slowly deteriorated,
draining the joy from my life."

It might be easy to conclude that Erin was just bummed because things
weren't going well for the team or something. Sure, she was racking up individual honors, but maybe UCSB was a bummer of a basketball team.

Maybe that's why she seemed to be enjoying it so little.

Not exactly. The Gauchos climbed to a top-ten ranking in the country.
They won the Big West Conference each year she was there. Oh, yes, and
Buescher was MVP of the league in all three of those seasons.

"I never felt emptier," she explained. "Things looked good on the outside, but on the inside I was dying. I knew I wouldn't be able to last much longer. I knew I needed a change."

So what does a college basketball star do after her junior year when she doesn't want to keep playing for her school? Petition the WNBA for the right to enter the draft, right? Or perhaps take her MVP trophies and All-American status and transfer to someplace like Connecticut or Tennessee?

Not Erin Buescher. Remember, she wasn't looking for ink in *Sports Illustrated* or face time on *SportsCenter*. She was looking for her lost joy.

So she did what few if any big-time college athletes had ever done before. She left UCSB and transferred to a small Christian college that competed in the National Intercollegiate Athletic Association—the NAIA. She decided that she wanted to take her prodigious skills and her troubled heart to The Master's College, a California school with a whopping student enrollment that didn't even top the one-thousand mark. It'd be like Dwyane Wade announcing that next year he'd like to play in the CBA.

While Erin was following her heart—searching for the elusive joy that had been her trademark earlier in her sports career—everyone else seemed to think she had made a huge mistake.

"Everyone told me I would never play in the WNBA," Buescher recalls. "They said I was making the biggest mistake of my life, and that I would regret it forever. They told me I was not strong enough to handle the pressure; that I was running away.

"That was hard to swallow, since I knew it wasn't the truth. I wasn't running from anything; I felt like I was running *to* God. I was at total peace about it, and if I didn't play professionally because of seeking Him, that was fine."

Buescher's move to The Master's College had the desired effect. She regained her desire to follow God more closely. "When you put yourself in that environment," she told the *Minnesota Christian Chronicle*, "it's inevitable that you're going to grow."

Perhaps part of the explanation for the reason Buescher needed a change so much is in her continual need to be associated with other believers. Part of the joy of being Erin Buescher is sharing the joy of being a Christian.

"I cannot emphasize enough how important the contact with other believers is," she says. "God calls us sheep for a reason. They roam in flocks; when they stray out away from the group alone, they are in much more danger than when they are in the midst of other sheep.

"The strength and power of numbers is amazing. I have grown to realize at a different level how, alone, it is extremely difficult to stay strong and aware. The Lord has been sweet in providing fellowship pretty much wherever I've gone, but I had to put out the effort to go and find the other believers wherever I am."

After playing that senior year at The Master's College, those naysayers about her WNBA career were proved wrong when she was drafted by the Minnesota Lynx. That was in 2001. She spent one year with the Lynx, then the next two seasons in Charlotte with the Sting. In 2004, she did not play in the WNBA. But 2005 found her in Sacramento, playing for the Monarchs.

Who knew what God had in store for her there? After all, she has learned through all of her circumstances that there's only one way to find joy. "It's amazing how without fail, He will provide me with the comfort, assurance, peace, and contentment I need. It's frustrating that I find myself so many times in life trying to find these things through other avenues, and every time it's a dead end drawing me back to the only true Source."

Oh, and there was a little added bonus in the California state capital for Erin and her new teammates.

The Sacramento Monarchs surprised everybody by winning the WNBA title in the summer of 2005, and Erin Buescher, the small-college girl everyone had given up on, had her championship ring.

She played in twenty-three games for the Monarchs during the season but saw limited action during the playoffs.

Did that destroy her joy?

"As a competitor it is extremely hard to sit on the sidelines and watch the battle when you want so badly to be in there fighting alongside your teammates." Buescher says. "You work hard all year, every day in practice, work on your game, take care of your body, prepare for the games, and then to sit and watch the game go by without being able to contribute . . . Is that difficult? Extremely! What do you do?

"You find a way to cheer your heart out for your teammates who *are* in the battle—to support them, let them know you are behind them, wanting them to be successful, because when it comes down to it, we are a *team*.

"This isn't tennis, golf, or an individual sport. It's a team sport, and that means personal desires and wishes are secondary. I had to come to a place where I was able to accept (whether I agree or disagree) that the coach is going to do what he thinks will give us the highest chance to win. And I, under his authority, have to respect and support that. Is it easy? Not at all, but you know we had a team of thirteen unselfish people, which is why we won a championship, and I feel *totally* grateful to have been a part of that. And although I didn't play very many minutes, I still was a part of it."

Do you doubt the joy that Erin Buescher has rediscovered as she continues to play pro basketball, continues to search for ways to help her family reach their goal of becoming missionaries, and continues to trust God in every circumstance?

If you take a look at the team photo of the Monarchs celebrating their WNBA title, you'll find Erin by looking for the young woman with the biggest smile.

Looking Up

Did you ever notice how little fun some people seem to have when they are playing their sport? Perhaps they missed out on the part of that phrase that has the word "playing" in it. Some athletes seem so miserable, even though they are doing something that is supposed to be so much fun.

They scowl. They frown. They swear. They get angry about everything. And often these "players" are making millions of dollars to go out there—yet they still act like somebody just keyed their Bentley.

That's why it's so much fun to see athletes who clearly enjoy playing their sport. Magic Johnson was one of those players. So was Pete Maravich. More recently, David Robinson seemed to enjoy the experience. And Steve Nash is just simply having so much fun out there.

Now, let's apply that same kind of thinking to the church.

Did you ever notice how little fun some people seem to have when they are living the Christian life? Perhaps they missed out on the part where Jesus said that He gave life so it could be lived abundantly (read John 10:10). Some Christians seem so miserable, even though they have been given the best free gift ever known to man—eternal salvation.

They scowl. They frown. Well, maybe they don't swear. They are angry about everything—even other Christians.

That's why it's so much fun to see Christians who clearly enjoy living as Christ-followers. Erin Buescher is one of those people.

Perhaps you know Christians of both kinds: The ones who are so sour on life, they'll probably complain about the streets of gold being too slick, if there were to be complaining in heaven. And the ones who simply light up the room with their smile.

Which sounds like a better way to reflect the love of God to others? Which will please Him and enhance your relationship with the God of your salvation?

The Bible Addresses Joy

"For the kingdom of heaven is not a matter of eating and drinking, but of righteousness, peace and joy in the Holy Spirit." (Romans 14:17)

"The precepts of the Lord are right, giving joy to the heart." (Psalm 19:8)

"Many are asking, 'Who can show us any good?' Let the light of your face shine upon us, O Lord. You have filled my heart with greater joy than when their grain and new wine abound." (Psalm 4:6–7)

"May the God of hope fill you with all joy and peace as you trust in him, so that you may overflow with hope by the power of the Holy Spirit." (Romans 15:13)

Chris Paul

Honoring Those Older

Rise in the presence of the aged, show respect for the elderly
and revere your God.
—*Leviticus 19:32*

WHEN YOU'RE A HIGH SCHOOL SENIOR, there's a lot to love. Especially if you're a basketball star with unlimited potential and major college coaches sitting in your living room romancing your future.

You love wearing the uniform in front of the home fans.

You love the way the other kids (especially the young ladies) respect you.

You love walking down the street and having people say, "Is that. . . ?"

For NBA guard Chris Paul, there was one more object of his love while he was growing up in Lewisville, North Carolina, as a high school superstar: his grandfather, to whom he refers as Papa Chilly.

Nathaniel Jones was Chris's maternal grandfather, and he and Chris were very close. It was Papa Chilly who would say to Chris each time the youngster would ask his grandfather how things were going, "Just fine, Christopher Emmanuel Paul. Blessed and highly favored in the Lord."

Nathaniel Jones went to almost all of Chris's games in high school. Every Sunday after church at Dreamland Park Baptist Church, where he was a deacon, he would take the Paul family out for lunch.

"For a lot of people, their best friend is a neighbor or a classmate," Paul has said. "For me, it was my grandfather. He taught me to be thankful for everything I received and that God should always be first in your life, and then your family. I don't think anyone was as proud of me and my accomplishments as my granddad."

Because Chris's grandma, Rachel, had died about ten years earlier, Jones, age sixty-one, lived alone. He owned a service station, which gave him the independence he wanted and the income he needed. Nathaniel Jones was a pioneer, for he has been noted as the first African-American to own a service station in the state of North Carolina.

Besides his work at his Chevron station, the rest of Grandpa Chilly's energy went toward his church and his family—notably toward Chris.

In November 2002, when Chris was a senior in high school, the star point guard signed a letter of intent to play basketball at Wake Forest, and when he did, his grandfather was there—along with Chris's parents, Robin and Charles. After Chris inked his name to that valuable piece of paper, Papa Chilly put a Wake Forest hat on his grandson's head. He said he was going to buy season tickets.

Chris's older brother, C. J., was home as well—home from college at the University of South Carolina–Spartanburg. He and Papa Chilly had plans to go out to eat that weekend.

Nathaniel Jones, as usual, had plans, and they included his beloved grandsons. He had more wisdom to impart—more love to give.

But then a most horrible tragedy struck.

The day after Chris Paul signed to go to Wake Forest, a group of teenagers ruined Chris's dream of looking up into the stands and seeing his grandfather cheering him on. On that day, on November 15, 2002, those teens accosted Nathaniel Jones in the driveway of his own home, robbed him, and killed him.

A community was outraged. How could such a good person be so heartlessly killed?

And how could Chris Paul go on?

He decided to go on by paying tribute to his grandfather.

Not much later, Chris Paul put on a high school basketball uniform for the first time in the new season. It was the first game of his senior year—and the first one he would have to play without his beloved grandfather watching.

The family had been talking about how to pay tribute to Papa Chilly. Chris had been having a hard time even leaving the family home, but he knew he wanted to do something special. An aunt had an idea, and she mentioned it to Chris's parents. They talked him into trying it.

Paul's school was playing against Parkland, the school attended by the boys who killed Papa Chilly, and that night Chris decided that the best way to honor his grandfather was to do it with a basketball in his hands. As he awaited the game, he was filled with more than the usual nervous anticipation.

"Before the game, my heart was racing. I knew I wanted to do something special for him. The hardest thing was to get back on the court and play. My family told me to be strong and that my grandfather wanted me to play."

Although Chris's highest previous output in a game was thirty-nine points, he easily surpassed that number in that memorable first game of his senior year. Battling back the tears from a heart broken by his grandpa's passing and working hard to overcome his sadness, he scored sixty-one points that night—one point for each of the years his grandpa had on this earth.

After he got point number sixty-one, Chris Paul stood at the free-throw line with a chance to make it number sixty-two. He air-balled the free throw attempt. As the West Forsyth fans stood to their feet in a standing ovation, Chris walked over to the bench and finally allowed himself to burst into tears. Appropriately for young Chris, his father, Charles, an assistant coach for the team, was there to hug him as he cried.

Chris Paul, just a teenager, had been wise enough to bestow on his grandfather the best honor he could think of by paying him tribute with one point for each year of his life. How better to honor one older and wiser than to show respect for combined value of the years he has served God on earth.

Looking Up

Age doesn't mean as much in twenty-first-century American culture as it once did. After all, when rock stars in their sixties are still performing music from their twenties, something has changed. Baby boomers who are entering their retirement years are still tooling around in Ford Mustangs and playing hockey.

It might be just a little more difficult for you to show proper respect for the "elderly" when they are busy downloading Beatles music onto their iPods and spending their discretionary income to try to look like they are thirty-five again. Yet changes in culture don't diminish scriptural truth. You need to respect those who have put more miles on their life's odometer.

Peter, writing to leaders in the church of his day, said in 1 Peter 5:5, "Young men, in the same way be submissive to those who are older." Proverbs 16:31 tells us that those who have reached the age at which their hair is turning gray have been given a "crown of glory." Job 12:12 mentions that those with a few extra years under their belt have an extra measure of wisdom.

So where does that leave you? As Chris Paul did, honor those special servants of God who have been around for a while and have earned that "crown." Whether you have a Grandpa Chilly in your life or not, you can always find someone older to show respect for and learn from.

It's the way God set things up, and just as Chris honored his granddad with sixty-one points, we should seek ways to give honor to whom honor is due.

The Bible Addresses Respect for Those Older

"Is not wisdom found among the aged? Does not long life bring understanding?" (Job 12:12)

"With long life will I satisfy him and show him my salvation." (Psalm 91:16)

"Gray hair is a crown of splendor; it is attained by a righteous life." (Proverbs 16:31)

"Even to your old age and gray hairs I am he, I am he who will sustain you." (Isaiah 46:4)

31

Danny Wuerffel
The Right Role Model

Let another praise you, and not your own mouth.
—*Proverbs 27:2*

ROLE MODELS. SOME PEOPLE DON'T PUT much
stock in the whole idea.

You might remember that Charles Barkley famously declared in a television commercial that he was not one. Of course, the Round Mound of Rebound was just reading words off a cue card, and who knows if he meant it or not. Matter of fact, who can tell when Charles is serious or just blowing smoke? Regardless, it's not unusual for big-time athletes to deny that responsibility.

There is a certain fear involved in the whole idea of saying that you want people to look at you and model themselves after you. In one sense, it could be prideful to suggest that your life is worth emulating.

Yet if an athlete does it right—if he or she deflects the adoration toward the right source of light and if he or she compels younger fans to appreciate the source of that talent and not just the talent, then there is hope for role models to make a difference.

Which brings us to Danny Wuerffel.

At one time during his football career, Wuerffel had every reason in the world to think of himself more highly than he ought (see Romans 12:3). After all, among the thousands of college athletes who played NCAA in 1996, Danny Wuerffel was voted the very best player. He was handed the Heisman Trophy for his work as quarterback of the Florida Gators.

Also living in Florida at the time was a little kid whose parents wanted him to look up to the right kind of people. This was a Christian family—a missionary family, actually—and they wanted their little boy, Timmy, to follow in the footsteps of someone who loved Jesus, who stayed humble, and who played some pretty good football.

So little Timmy was encouraged to look up to Wuerffel as his role model. Not only did Timmy get a chance to see Wuerffel in action on the gridiron, but he also got the thrilling opportunity to meet him in person.

Wuerffel, who took every opportunity he could get to speak in churches and work with young people as a young football star, visited Timmy's church on a couple of occasions to speak.

Big stars can have big heads. They can overlook how much they influence others with their words and their actions.

At about the same time Danny Wuerffel was visiting Timmy's church in Jacksonville, Florida, a big-time NBA star was visiting a basketball tournament near Grand Rapids, Michigan. When he did, he met privately with some of the people who had brought him to the tournament. Informally, the big star and the people who brought him got together for lunch and a rest from being surrounded by adoring fans.

With that group was a youngster, a kid about the same age as Timmy. That kid, named Steve, saw a big star who didn't seem to understand completely the role-model thing.

"Can we have a couple of pictures?" he was asked.

"No. No cameras, please."

"Oh, okay. How about an autograph?"

Again, "No. I don't want to get started with that."

There were only about eight people in the room—including one very disappointed youngster who didn't quite know what to think of a man who wouldn't get his picture taken with him and wouldn't even sign an autograph.

In Jacksonville, Florida, though, when Timmy approached Danny Wuerffel and asked for his autograph, the best player in college football was more than happy to oblige. Didn't matter that signing one autograph meant signing many, many more.

That's what humility does. It reminds a person that he's not too good to help a nine-year-old kid.

So who was that kid named Timmy, and why did it make any difference at all that Danny Weurffel treated him so well?

Turns out the kid would be a star in his own right. Timmy grew up to be Tim Tebow—a young man who would play college football on the same field as Danny Wuerffel for the Florida Gators.

Pam Tebow talked about the difference the older quarterback made in her son's life.

"Danny Wuerffel taught him a lot about humility. He always deflected praise, and he never acted like he was better than other people. Those are the kinds of things we taught our boys. Danny was a hero for Timmy. He was a wonderful role model, and he never disappointed us."

What Wuerffel brings to those around him is best exemplified by his chosen vocation after his NFL career ended. While many seek further fame or recognition through myriad positions of power and prestige, Wuerffel and his wife, Jessica, turned themselves over to God as servants. They poured themselves into a ministry to struggling teenagers in New Orleans—kids with nowhere to go but down.

The Wuerffels settled in New Orleans and began working with Desire Street Ministries—working closely with kids from troubled homes and situations that seemed hopeless. Content to give their lives to these kids, Danny and Jessica didn't know that their commitment would end up costing them their home as well.

When Katrina tore through the Gulf Coast, it hit the Wuerffels' home. It damaged Desire Street Ministries, making it unlivable for a long time. So what did the Wuerffels do? They helped move the kids and everything to Florida. Through his contacts, Wuerffel obtained a campground where Desire Street could start up again while waiting to see if they could return to New Orleans.

The more people observe of Wuerffel, the more they want to honor him. Think, for instance, of what the All Sports Association has done. In order to honor the college football player whom they feel best exemplifies a combination of athletic prowess, community services, and academic success, they created the Danny Wuerffel Trophy—kind of a good-guy Heisman Trophy.

Longtime college coach-turned ESPN football analyst Bill Curry, like Wuerffel, a Christian, said of the award: "This award is not just a little different from all the other awards, it's a lot different. When I was approached about this, I was a little skeptical, until I realized it was the embodiment of everything that Danny Wuerffel stands for. The spirit of this award is something that is long overdue. You're recognizing not only a great athlete and a great student but someone who also gives and gives."

You don't have to be an active NFL player to be a role model, and

Wuerffel is definitely not shirking from that role now that he's done with playing football on Sundays.

Whether he's helping the kids at Desire Street or working with adults who want to help support the ministry, he knows people are still watching, and he's willing to let them watch him serve Jesus in new and varied ways.

Like a true role model.

Looking Up

The apostle Paul had a pretty good idea of what a role model was, even if he never heard of the idea.

In 1 Corinthians, he made it clear that if the folks at Corinth were having a hard time finding someone to emulate (and with the problems they were experiencing, that seemed to be the case), they could follow him. But on one condition.

Here's what Paul said in 1 Corinthians 10:31–32: "So whether you eat or drink or whatever you do, do it all for the glory of God. Do not cause anyone to stumble, whether Jews, Greeks, or the church of God." Okay, that set up the standard: Do everything for God and don't bring anyone down with your sin.

But Paul went further than just telling people what to do.

"Even as I try to please everybody in every way . . ." he goes on, explaining his own desire to be an encouragement to others. "For I am not seeking my own good but the good of many, so that they may be saved." The example—the role model—is being set.

Then this: "Follow my example, as I follow the example of Christ" (1 Corinthians 11:1).

To be a role model—to live in a way that leads others to Jesus—Paul seemed to be saying there is one main criteria: "Follow me only if I follow Christ."

A true Christian role model, then, is a person who lives as best he or she can the way Jesus lived. Jesus, who showed humility by coming to earth. Jesus, who showed trust by being born into a poor family. Jesus, who showed love by feeding the hungry and healing the sick. Jesus, who suffered without complaint and sacrificed himself completely.

Want to be a role model now? It's tough work, but Paul says it's possible.

And worth the effort.

The Bible Addresses Examples

"Be perfect, therefore, as your heavenly Father is perfect." (Matthew 5:48)

"Don't let anyone look down on you because you are young, but set an example for the believers in speech, in life, in love, in faith and in purity." (1 Timothy 4:12)

"In everything set them an example by doing what is good." (Titus 2:7)

"Brothers, as an example of patience in the face of suffering, take the prophets." (James 5:10)

Curt Schilling
On the Wings of Prayer

Be joyful in hope, patient in affliction, faithful in prayer.
—*Romans 12:12*

THE BOSTON RED SOX SURPRISED BASEBALL
fans in a brand-new way in 2004. The denizens of Fenway Park, one of the
most storied and hallowed sports venues in North America, put the finishing
touches on the best baseball story of the year and one of the best of all-time
by doing something no one had ever done in baseball history. In doing so,
they simultaneously erased a troubling pattern that had stretched across
more than eighty seasons.

That year, the New York Yankees beat the Red Sox in the first two
games of the American League Championship Series. In the third contest,
the Yanks again came out on top, this time obliterating the BoSox 19–8 to
take a 3–0 lead in the series. It appeared that for the eighty-sixth straight
season, Fenway Park would go through another winter of discontent. Once
more, it seemed, the mighty Yankees would have their way with the
beloved, beleaguered Boston Red Sox.

The Fenway faithful welcomed the Red Sox back home for Game Four,
hoping against hope for a miracle. Chances of that seemed slim as the Red
Sox came to bat in the bottom of the ninth. New York held a 4–3 lead as
the Sox stepped in to face arguably the best relief pitcher of all-time, Mari-
ano Rivera. A walk to Kevin Millar put pinch-runner Dave Roberts on first.
He stole second and scored on a single by Bill Mueller. In the twelfth
inning, David Ortiz blasted a long home run that gave life to the Red Sox.
Game Five also went to the Red Sox in extra innings, which left things up
to Curt Schilling in Game Six.

That's when baseball fans all across North America found out for the
first time what kind of man Curt Schilling really was. First, they discovered
a man of incredible courage and tenacity. And then they discovered the surprising source of those traits.

That Schilling pitched at all that day is a story in and of itself. He had
been suffering from an ankle injury that should have left him in street
clothes for Game Five. The tendons surrounding the outside of his right

ankle were dislocated. Before the game, team physicians tried to cobble Schilling back together by putting some stitches in his ankle to keep it from unraveling completely.

So held together by thread, Schilling took to the mound in the Sox' third attempt to stave off elimination. With his foot bleeding through the sanitary socks that he wore under his red stirrups and with the pain never relenting, Schilling allowed the Yankees just four hits in seven innings of work, and Boston won Game Six 4–2 to earn a Game Seven showdown.

Throughout the game, fans marveled at Schilling's ability to perform so well under such duress. In normal circumstances, he should not have been able to walk, let alone pitch in one of the most important games in Red Sox history.

Then after the game, fans were let in on something that many of them did not know. Curt Schilling's dependence during this game was not just on the stitching in his ankle—his true dependence was on prayers to His Father in heaven.

Kenny Albert, Fox TV reporter, helped let the world in on the spiritual secret to Schilling's success when he asked the veteran pitcher how he had been able to do so well despite the obstacles.

"It's all right. I became a Christian seven years ago, and I have never in my life been touched by God like I was tonight."

Surprisingly, Fox didn't cut away to a commercial. They let Schilling keep talking.

"I tried to go out and do it myself in Game One, and you saw what happened. [Schilling lost.] Tonight was God's night, no question."

Later he said, "I just wanted to, in the end, be able to go out and compete and pitch. I could not do that on my own. The prayers that I usually pray are nothing more than allowing me to glorify His name." And that prayer was definitely answered.

For perhaps the first time in his career, Schilling was using his platform as a superstar pitcher to explain the value of prayer and faith while facing a tough situation.

Schilling was not done with prayer and faith.

The Red Sox, as everyone who doesn't live in Borneo knows by now, won Game Seven and went on to face the St. Louis Cardinals in the World

Series. Schilling was slated to pitch Game Two.

Of course, his ankle was still a mess.

"When I woke up that morning in agony, I called the team doctors and trainers and told them I was not going to be able to pitch," Schilling recalls. "I walked into the clubhouse and they took the suture out that punctured my nerve. Things started to get better."

Yet as game-time drew near, Schilling began to wonder if he could pull it off one more time. "The magnitude of what I was trying to get ready to do hit me. I knew I was pushing the limit. I was pitching my last game of the year."

Because of his pregame workout, Schilling had missed chapel, so he went to his teammate and fellow Christian Trot Nixon and asked him to get chaplain Walt Day for him.

"I felt like I was walking with a five-hundred-pound bag of sand on my shoulders. I sat down next to Walt, and he asked me what I wanted him to do. I just broke down into tears. I said, 'I just want you to pray that I can glorify God and compete tonight.'"

Schilling told Day, "I don't feel worthy. After all the things I've done wrong in my life, all the things I've said and thought, I don't deserve this."

Day answered, "That's why the Lord put His Son on the cross."

And Day prayed for his friend . . .

Curt Schilling.

You can say what you want about tradition and defeating the curse and the label "Idiots" the Boston Red Sox put on themselves. Any and all of these ideas—at least psychologically—aided the Boston Red Sox as they marched toward World Series glory. But Curt Schilling will unashamedly come back with a different explanation.

"God did something amazing," he says of this ability to pitch on a bum ankle. "I went to the Lord for help because I knew I was not going to be able to do this myself."

While the victory of the Red Sox certainly deserves notice as a remarkable feat, it should also be noted that Schilling's careful and faithful revelation that he depended on God for help through prayer had its effect as well.

It's kind of nice that a long-standing problem that had been for decades attributed to a curse ended up being a true blessing—in part because of one man's prayerfulness.

Looking Up

There's prayer, and there is prayerfulness.

Although we can't say that one will work while one won't, it seems that an attitude of prayerfulness corresponds with what God expects from us.

Prayer: "God, help me today."

Prayerfulness: "Lord, it's me again. I know this is the thirteenth time I've talked with you today, but I don't want you to overlook my request. It's very important, and I think your name will be glorified through the answer you give."

Prayer is getting a sip from a fountain.

Prayerfulness is ordering a Big Gulp and downing the whole thing. Then getting another one.

In a parable told by Jesus in the New Testament (Luke 18), the indication seems to be that Jesus would prefer that we go the Big Gulp route and not use the little sip method of prayer.

Here's what happened. A town had a judge who was not easy to get along with. He didn't fear God and he didn't have much love for people. One day a widow came to the judge and asked for some justice. She was all alone in the world, and her only possible advocate could be the judge.

But not this one.

He kept saying no to her request for justice.

And she kept asking, brave woman that she was.

So guess what? The nasty judge finally gave in to her—not because of his moral character, which was deficient, but because of her insistence.

Jesus used that story to tell His listeners not to stop praying. If an unjust judge will give in, how much more will a just and righteous God answer the continued requests of His children.

Once and done doesn't do it. Prayerfulness does. Let's show God how much we trust Him by practicing prayerfulness.

The Bible Addresses Prayerfulness

"Pray continually." (1 Thessalonians 5:17)

"The prayer of a righteous man is powerful and effective." (James 5:16)

"I love the Lord, for he heard my voice; he heard my cry for mercy. Because he turned his ear to me, I will call on him as long as I live." (Psalm 116:1–2)

"The Lord is near to all those who call on him, to all who call on him in truth." (Psalm 145:18)

Luke Ridnour
Stepping Up

For God did not give us a spirit of timidity, but a spirit of power,
of love and of self-discipline.
—*2 Timothy 1:7*

LUKE RIDNOUR WAS NO LEBRON JAMES. He
didn't burst on the scene out of high school to crash the NBA at age eighteen and turn it on its ear by being among the best players in the league while the ink on his diploma was still wet.

And Luke Ridnour was no Dwight Howard, who told the world before he even entered the NBA that one of the main reasons he was suiting up in the best basketball league in the world was so he could spread the gospel of Jesus Christ.

In both basketball maturity and spiritual boldness, Ridnour was a little slower than those two younger players. Yet basketball life and the Christian life are not always about comparisons. Instead, they are about taking what you have and maximizing it to the greatest possible potential.

Ridnour entered the NBA in 2003—the same year LeBron James graduated from high school and was the first pick in the draft. Luke himself went to the league early, leaving the University of Oregon after his junior year and ending up near home with the Seattle SuperSonics. His maturation as a guard in the rough-and-tumble NBA was slow, but by the end of his second season, his growth as a player had some whispering the name "Steve Nash" when they spoke of the eventual heights to which Ridnour could aspire as a player.

But this is not about basketball. It is about faith. And it is the story of how Luke Ridnour shot up spiritually after matriculating in the NBA. That is not always how it happens with kids who grow up in the church, go away to college and all of its temptations, then find themselves filthy rich before they are twenty-one years old. Many times the pro sports life saps the spiritual strength right out of these kids and starts them down a path that leads them further and further from God.

One NBA player, who started out his basketball career in a Christian school while a middle-schooler, drifted so far from his roots that by the time his career in the league reached its final years, he had become a tragic figure noted more for failed expectations than for fulfilling God's—or even man's—purposes for him.

No one ever expected that kind of demise for Luke, but perhaps no one expected the way he escalated his faith and dependence on God while taking his game to another level either. After all, Luke became a Christian as a youngster of five, and throughout his rise to prominence, he continued to emphasize matters of faith.

But as Ridnour approached the third season of his NBA career, something changed.

The change began for the Seattle point guard when he decided that all of the free time and down time that was his while the team was on the road could be put to good use. Of course, that unaccounted-for time has been the demise of many pro athletes, so it's good to find out that this pro athlete was not about to take the wrong path.

"God began to truly teach me from His Word," Ridnour told *Sports Spectrum* magazine writer Jeanne Halsey about the extra time he spent reading his Bible as his team traveled away from Seattle.

The more he studied, the more he was convinced that God had put him in the spotlight of the NBA so he could reflect that light back on His Savior.

"He has put me in this place, in this mission field, to be His speaker." Ridnour concluded. And he decided that his speaking would be directed at both his NBA fellows and then the public at large.

For Ridnour, the reason for his spiritual growth and increase in boldness is clear. "That's what happens when the living Word of God becomes active in our hearts. The more we want to know about Him, the deeper we want our relationship with Him to grow."

Although Ridnour's climb up the spiritual ladder took an individual interest on his part, he was not alone in its genesis. He got some prodding from a Eugene, Oregon, pastor who had worked with him while he was starring as an Oregon Duck. Keith Jenkins was, as Ridnour explains, "my spiritual mentor."

After Jenkins lit the fire under Ridnour in college, his spiritual fervor grew into a flame after he moved up to the big time.

Nearly every Christian athlete who is written about by the secular press is given one automatic label that non-Christian writers think best summarizes what is going on with a sports star who also professes to believe in Jesus Christ.

"He got religion," uninitiated sportswriters will say. Or "He's really religious."

Problem is, they don't get what has really gone on. They don't understand that what happened to Luke Ridnour to move him closer to God and bolder in his faith was not some churchy thing like lighting a candle or mouthing a Gregorian chant.

Those knee-jerk scribes might be surprised to hear Luke say, "I'm not a religious person."

Say what? "Then what are you doing talking about God and all that Bible stuff?" they might ask.

Calmly, as if standing at the free-throw line with his 90-percent shooting stat in his arsenal, Ridnour would answer: "I'm a person who is in a relationship with God. He is the ruler of my life. He is truly my Father."

Then he would remind them that in religion, people do a lot of good things in order to try to get to heaven. But with Jesus, the work has already been done. "I want to tell them about Jesus, who died for them," he says.

Every professional athlete goes through stages in his career. Each strives to get better by working on weaknesses and listening to advice, because each player wants to reach the ultimate goal in his or her sport: the championship. Luke Ridnour is no exception. He would like nothing better than to use the talent he has developed since he was a little kid dribbling the ball along gravel roads in Blaine, Washington, to help his team hoist the Larry O'Brien NBA Championship trophy some late June night.

But Ridnour is also carrying with him an additional challenge—the challenge that comes from a heart on fire for God. "I want to talk about what God's doing in my life, because it is so exciting."

To that end, he has taken his faith to the streets as a part of Jammin' Against the Darkness, a celebration of music, basketball, and Jesus that happens in NBA arenas across the country. At those events, such as one at the Key Arena in Seattle in 2005, when more than five hundred kids walked down to the arena floor to pray to trust Jesus Christ, Ridnour shows that although he might not quite be a LeBron James-like superstar, he has something far more important to give kids than a new brand of sneaker. He has a genuine, explosive desire to make sure they know about eternal life.

It's the new Luke Ridnour, and it's refreshing. As he makes his way through an NBA career that puts him in the spotlight eighty-one times a year, he's also getting comfortable with shining that light on his heavenly Father. That's stepping up in a big way on the big stage.

Looking Up

Boldness in the faith, and the spiritual growth that fuels that boldness, were the marks of another guy with a pretty famous biblical name. A guy named Paul.

When a flash of light got Paul's attention and turned him from a Christian-bashing renegade into a Jesus-following disciple, he was immediately changed into a bold witness for the Lord. Yet he was not turned out onto the masses without some training. God directed Paul to go to a seminary of sorts—a three-year stay in Arabia. He had the boldness, but he also needed the guidance of both God's message and the Holy Spirit's strength.

We can look at Luke Ridnour and suppose that he's pretty bold already. After all, he has to go up against the likes of Allen Iverson, Steve Nash, and Dwyane Wade. That takes boldness.

But often for Christians, a boldness in school or on the job does not translate to boldness in the faith. That only comes when, as Luke did, we turn our attention to Scripture and let it instruct us.

Are we giving God a chance to change us—to embolden us? Do we spend enough time with an open Bible in front of us so that He can even show us what He wants us to know?

That's the challenge of spiritual growth, which leads to bravery in witnessing to others.

The Bible Addresses Spiritual Growth

"I pray that . . . Christ may dwell in your hearts through faith. And I pray that you, being rooted and established in love, may have power, together with all the saints, to grasp how wide and long and high and deep is the love of Christ." (Ephesians 3:16–18)

"For this very reason, make every effort to add to your faith goodness; and to goodness, knowledge; and to knowledge, self-control; and to self-control, persever-ance; and to perseverance, godliness; and to godliness, brotherly kindness; and to brotherly kindness, love. For if you possess these qualities in increasing measure, they will keep you from being ineffective and unproductive in your knowledge of our Lord Jesus Christ." (2 Peter 1:5–8)

"Grow in the grace and knowledge of our Lord and Savior Jesus Christ." (2 Peter 3:18)

Aaron Baddeley
Winning the Dating Game
I will instruct you and teach you in the way you should go.
—Psalm 32:8

JOSH HARRIS MADE A BIG SPLASH ON THE
scene among Christian teenagers in the mid 1990s with his book *I Kissed Dating Goodbye*. In that book, he gave his philosophy about how teen guys and girls should behave toward each other—including his thinking that dating is not a good idea.

Professional golfer Aaron Baddeley's approach to dating never made the bestseller list as did Harris's, but not because the two-time Australian Open winner didn't try to make his helpful approach well-known. He just used a different communication strategy.

Instead of putting his ideas in a book, Baddeley published his thoughts about dating on his Web site: *www.badds.com*. In an effort to encourage teenage Christians toward sexual purity, he dedicated a portion of his Web site to supplying biblical guidelines for dating.

So who is this Aaron Baddeley guy? As mentioned, he has had some golf success in Australia, and in fact, he has spent a lot of time Down Under. Although he was born in the United States, his family moved to Australia when he was young, so he grew up there.

He proved to be an excellent golfer, and by the time he was twenty, he had won the Australian Open golf tournament twice. In 2003, he joined the American PGA Tour full time, and he's been knocking golf balls around PGA tournament courses ever since.

With that little bit of history in mind, let's return to Aaron's philosophy on dating. Ironically (and this is ironic because of what happened to Aaron on April 19, 2005), Baddeley built the foundation of his philosophy on a verse of Scripture that says, "Seek not a wife." Yes, in the King James Version, that is exactly what Paul tells the people of Corinth in 1 Corinthians 7:27.

To Baddeley, that verse told him that as a young man he was to trust God in all things—even the choice of a wife. He felt that it was not his task to go on a hunting expedition to find the young woman of his dreams. No.

That task, he felt, was to be left up to God. If he would trust God, He would bring the right person to him.

Turns out, He did.

Her name is Richelle, and it was on April 19, 2005, that Aaron married Richelle Robbins in Scottsdale, Arizona. And to further illuminate Aaron's belief that God would direct him, it's important to note that they met on a blind date. Indeed, Aaron did not seek Richelle out—God directed them together.

Before that, though, Baddeley took what he called a Dating Vow and a Dating Fast.

During the Dating Vow time, Baddeley went six months without a one-on-one date. When he went out with girls, he went out in groups—never alone with one young lady. He called this time of non-dating an "act of obedience." He felt that instead of using up his time and effort on dates, he could improve his relationship with God. "Just think about how much energy is used up in a dating relationship," he said. "God wants us to use that energy to know Him better and serve Him.

"I don't want my seeking another person to hinder [my relationship with God] and drive me further from Him," Baddeley explained.

During the Dating Fast, the golfer used the time he would normally be on dates to pray and read God's Word. He felt the trade-off of being with God instead of with girls improved his relationship with God.

There's something else Baddeley did during his pre-marriage days that reminded him of the seriousness of preserving purity in his relationship with girls as a way to preserve intimacy in relationship with God.

He wore a purity ring on the finger most often reserved for a wedding ring. It was a silver piece of jewelry, and it had a cross etched in it. Many people noticed the ring, thinking it was a wedding band. But it wasn't there to confuse others. It was there as a constant reminder to Aaron that his real purpose in life was to please God and live for Him. And sexual purity was indeed one key way to do that.

But let's back up a little here. There had to be a time when he put his Dating Vow and Dating Fast behind him—otherwise he would never have been able to win Richelle's heart. Truth is, Aaron Baddeley is not actually anti-dating. In fact, he describes the first time he and Richelle spent considerable time together as their "first date."

They went out for dinner, and then they talked for three hours, Baddeley relates.

The key, Baddeley contends, is not to avoid dating—except for those special Vow and Fast times. No, as dating happens with a special person, the key, he says, is keeping Christ at the center of the relationship. He readily admits that temptation arises in dating situations, but he also suggests that standing by godly principles will keep Christians away from sin.

"My motto is, 'You should only go as far as you're comfortable telling your parents about.'"

"God doesn't want to hinder relationships," Baddeley declares. "He wants to help them and take away the pain."

So now, as Baddeley enjoys his life as a professional golfer, he is able to share his adventure with a young lady who shares his faith and his goal of bringing honor to God in everything.

Clearly, that makes Aaron and Richelle winners of the dating game.

Looking Up

Arranged marriages. That doesn't sound like much fun.

One day Dad comes home from work, and with him is a guy who looks as if he missed all the important meetings in health class. His clothes suggest that he's spent too much time playing video games to notice the latest fashions.

Yet Dad likes this guy, and he wants you, his teenage daughter, to meet him. Dad somehow thinks this is the guy you should be interested in. Dad thinks this is, well, *the* guy.

That's not the way to win friends and influence daughters. Nobody wants Dad to pick her boyfriend. That's even worse than letting the fans pick the NBA All-Star team.

Yet there is one Father who should be the One putting people together. His name is Jehovah, and He has the right to provide that guidance.

In fact, He has already provided some guidance for any person looking for a lifetime partner. For instance, Scripture says that Christians should not "be yoked together with unbelievers" (2 Corinthians 6:14). Also, young men need to stay pure, and they do that by "living according to [God's] Word"

(Psalm 119:9). Further, young men who are seeking God's best for them will listen to the advice of older, wiser believers: "Young men . . . be submissive to those who are older" (1 Peter 5:5).

Living by God's principles and then trusting God's guidance are the best ways to find a future mate. If those ideals are upheld, then whatever method a young person decides on—dating, courting, or just waiting for God to lead—he or she can have confidence in God's leading.

The Bible Addresses Guidance

"The plans of the Lord stand firm forever." (Psalm 33:11)

"All the days ordained for me were written in your book." (Psalm 139:16)

"Whether you turn to the right or to the left, your ears will hear a voice behind you, saying, 'This is the way; walk in it.'" (Isaiah 30:21)

Tim Howard

The Power to Overcome

There was given me a thorn in my flesh.
—2 Corinthians 12:7

HOW HE DID IT WAS ANYONE'S GUESS. Clearly, this was not what anyone suspected would ever happen.

Kids growing up in North Brunswick, New Jersey, simply do not lie awake at night trying to figure out how they will someday wear a soccer jersey that has the emblem of Manchester United on it.

New York Jets, maybe.

New York Yankees, for sure.

New York Knicks, yes.

MetroStars, certainly.

But Manchester United? It probably sounds to a lot of kids like the Methodist church down on the corner instead of the world's most famous soccer team.

And if they have heard of it, what kid striving to play college soccer or even Major League Soccer could think he has a shot at playing soccer where soccer is king?

So the fact that North Brunswick's own Tim Howard landed a spot on the most well-known team in the Premier League will always be a source of wonderment.

Howard himself called it "just as much a shock to me as anyone else."

After Howard had played in the MLS for a few years, scouts for Man U started eyeing the talented goalkeeper. They watched him perform for the MetroStars for a couple of years, and then came the surprise call: Man U wants you!

When Howard crossed the ocean to play soccer in England, he discovered the sport was a bit different there. For one thing, the pressure was more intense.

"It's difficult to describe," he says. "There's always somebody waiting in the wings to take your place. You go out in front of seventy thousand people every weekend, without fail. That pressure can get to you if you're not grounded and focused."

That grounding is part of what Howard called "an awesome adventure that God had planned." He and his wife, Laura, had already decided that they were going to trust God's plan for them. "I guess we learned that God's rule is sovereign. Coming to England, we saw how He touched people's lives. You see God's power and presence everywhere, even an ocean away."

But while Howard discovered some things that were different from playing in the U.S., one thing seemed to be the same: The media who wrote about him didn't always get it right. And some didn't have quite the sensitivity that he would like.

See, there's something about Tim Howard that hasn't been mentioned yet, and although Howard has worked to make sure it's not a defining characteristic, it still affects how people perceive him. That something is called Tourette's syndrome. This condition, which affects people in varying degrees, is sometimes marked by uncontrollable tics or by saying things at inappropriate times without being able to control it.

Howard was first diagnosed with Tourette's when he was ten, and they told him it was a mild case, which it has been.

While he had help in trying to cope with the reality of having this condition, which can become debilitating, he also discovered that faith was a factor in dealing with it. "I had fought for years trying to accept it on my own and let other people know I had it," Howard says.

"But when you accept Christ, His mercy and grace are so powerful that you can't help but look at yourself and accept yourself for everything you are. It meant no longer having any physical or mental shackles."

However, when Howard began playing soccer in England, he discovered that the writers didn't quite understand that concept. When the writers in England found out he had Tourette's, they hauled out their laptops.

"The tabloid papers had written quite ignorant articles about it," Howard recalls. "But I didn't read them. I tend to block them out, and I don't think anything about it. I feel comfortable in my own skin. I'm happy with the way God made me."

That has proved to be the best way for Howard to work through being a high-profile player with a problem that many don't understand. Being happy with the way God made him has allowed him to "let my faith guide me by putting my trust in Him."

In addition, accepting himself has allowed Howard to be of help to others, especially kids, who struggle with Tourette's syndrome. One time, while still playing for the MetroStars, Howard invited more than one hundred children with Tourette's to watch one of his games. Then, after the game, he hung around for more than two hours to answer any questions the kids' parents might have for him.

Howard's former teammate with the MetroStars best summed up the way Howard has overcome his difficulty: "Some people say Tim *suffers from* Tourette's syndrome," said Steve Shak. "But the way I see it, the world has been a better place because Tim *successfully lives with* Tourette's syndrome."

Looking Up

Athletes are supposed to be the people with the flawless physiques, the incredible strength, and the matchless physical ability. They are the ones who are invincible—somehow above the fray when it comes to the ailments that touch most of our lives.

But occasionally we meet athletes who must not only overcome the odds of being professional athletes but also overcome illnesses or disabilities that would keep the rest of us out of action.

Jim Abbott, for example, was a major league baseball player despite having been born with just one hand.

Clay Dyer is a professional fisherman although he was born with just one arm and no legs.

Jean Driscoll had spina bifida, yet she became the greatest wheelchair marathon racer in the world in the 1990s.

These people are inspiring because they recognized that instead of moaning and complaining about what God had handed them, they worked doubly hard to become everything they could be.

The Bible tells us about some people who didn't have all the tools but who succeeded anyway. Moses was like that. He was slow of speech, yet he became a leader of millions. And Paul, the great apostle, had an unnamed problem that he asked God to take away from him three times.

But God doesn't always relieve us of physical difficulties. Sometimes He allows us to keep them so we can cling to His power. Scripture tells us that when we are weak, then God is strong.

The Lord told Paul, in connection with his malady, "My grace is sufficient for you, for my power is made perfect in weakness" (2 Corinthians 12:9).

Are you struggling because you have a weakness that continues to hamper your life? Do what Paul did: Ask God to take it from you, and then trust Him no matter how He answers. Demonstrate trust in the One who cares so much for you.

The Bible Addresses Troubles

"We also rejoice in our sufferings, because we know that suffering produces perseverance." (Romans 5:3)

"For our light and momentary troubles are achieving for us an eternal glory that far outweighs them all." (2 Corinthians 4:17)

"Endure hardship with us like a good soldier of Christ Jesus." (2 Timothy 2:3)

"Blessed is the man who perseveres under trial." (James 1:12)